An Occasional Cow

Polly Horvath

An Occasional Cow

Pictures by Gioia Fiammenghi

Published by The Trumpet Club
666 Fifth Avenue, New York, New York 10103

Text © 1989 by Polly Horvath
Pictures © 1989 by Gioia Fiammenghi

ISBN 0-440-84756-7

This edition published by arrangement with
Farrar, Straus and Giroux
Printed in the United States of America
January 1992

1 3 5 7 9 10 8 6 4 2
OPM

For my father and mother

Contents

An Occasional Cow

Mrs. Spark's Brainstorm

Summer was coming to New York. To Imogene, summer had come to mean one thing—wallets. Every year Mr. and Mrs. Spark sent Imogene to camp, where Imogene, who was not of an athletic persuasion, secluded herself in the crafts room and, under the cheerful direction of some bouncing counselor, produced wallet after wallet all summer long. It was better than school, Imogene decided, but not much.

She was walking home from her last day in school. The streets in mid-June were already beginning to smell like garbage. She liked this time in New York. Everyone looked hot and tired and crabby, but Madison Avenue was as colorful and varied as a circus. Purple, yellow, green, red, pink, white, and blazing floral clothes flipped past her. Imogene was trying to keep cool by walking in the shadow of a large, tired-looking man as he trundled up the avenue. When he turned off at East Sixty-second Street, Imogene glanced around for another gentleman with an equally obliging shadow and settled instead on a fat pinkish woman being led by a poodle. Imogene liked to see the chic ladies with fat, freckled arms poking out of their summer dresses. At East Seventieth, she left the woman and climbed upstairs to her apartment.

Her mother met her at the door, looking distracted. Her father was sitting on the couch, sipping a drink and playing with the ice cubes in his mouth—something Imogene had been told never to do. Imogene commented on this, but it went unnoticed.

Something, thought Imogene, is up.

"Imogene," said her mother, "we've just received some very unfortunate news."

"Yeah, I'll say," said her father.

"It concerns your camp, dear."

"Yeah, I'll say," said her father.

"It seems there was a fire," her mother continued.

"Yeah, I'll say," said her father.

"Oh, really, Henry!" her mother turned, annoyed. Mr. Spark spit his ice cubes back into the glass, something Imogene had been taught never, ever to do. She decided that this news must be serious indeed.

"And they've closed down the camp for the summer."

"Hoopla!" Imogene tried to imagine a summer without wallets—a whole summer in the city. It was beyond her.

"We tried to phone some other camps, but it's just too late in the season," said her mother.

Better and better, thought Imogene.

"So I had a little brainstorm, darling. Naturally, we don't want you to spend the summer in New York."

"Oh," said Imogene. "Does that mean that we're all going to rent a cottage on the ocean?" This was her favorite fantasy.

"Now, sweetheart," said her father, "you know your mother and I cannot take a whole summer off from work."

"Why not?" asked Imogene, who always felt like being disagreeable when her parents became patient and reasonable.

"We thought you might enjoy meeting your Iowa cousins," continued her mother. "So we called your Aunt Bobo, and she's invited you to spend the summer with them on their farm."

"Aunt Bobo?" whispered Imogene.

"Yes," said her mother.

"Iowa?" she squeaked.

"Yes," said her mother, continuing with her it's-all-settled air. "Won't it be nice to be near a lake, right out in the country? Cousin Josephine is just your age. Daddy and I will call you every week, and I'm sure you'll have a marvelous time."

Imogene's stomach dropped. She tried to remember

what she had learned about Iowa in school, but all she could think of was corn and pigs. She saw herself living in a tiny sod house completely engulfed by pig-ridden cornfields.

Her parents looked at her expectantly.

"No, thank you," she said firmly.

"What?" asked her parents.

"I don't want to go to Iowa. I don't know anybody in Iowa. Let's give this some more thought."

"It's all been arranged, dear," said her mother mildly. "I'm sure, if you consider carefully, you'll see what a lovely adventure this could be for you."

"Keep an, ahem, open mind," said her father, poking furtively in the ice bucket and not looking at her.

"That's right," chorused her mother with, Imogene felt, an annoying solidarity. "Heavens, I wish I could go with you. I haven't seen my cousin Bobo since I was a girl. We used to have wonderful times together. Every year we say we're going to get together, but we never do. She's so excited to meet you, Imogene. I've told her all about you."

"Why don't you come with me?" suggested Imogene.

"Be reasonable," said her mother in what Imogene knew was a warning tone.

She felt like saying a bad word. Loudly. Instead, she marched to the kitchen, poured herself a tall glass

of lemonade, and, grabbing the cookie jar, tramped upstairs to her bedroom and slammed the door.

She ate several cookies, but they were as chalk in
her mouth. It was bad enough to be going to Iowa, but
to spend the summer with a lot of aunts, uncles, and
cousins she had never met, who in any case were to be
distrusted because they chose to live in Iowa—well, that
was the limit.

She opened her bedroom door quietly. Her parents
were having cocktails and being very jolly in the living
room, completely oblivious to the sad fate of their one
and only child. "Humph," snorted Imogene. She would
call her cousins and thank them for their kind invitation
and refuse it civilly. She crept stealthily into her father's
study for the telephone. Her parents went right on drinking and laughing. She got out her father's file of phone
numbers and flipped through it until she found BUD AND
BOBO REINSTEIN. She had never made a long-distance
phone call before, but this was an emergency. She dialed
1 and then the Reinsteins' number. Then she hung up
and took several quick breaths. She dialed again. This
time she let it ring.

"Hello!" boomed a big voice.

"Hello?" said Imogene uncertainly. "Could I speak
to Josephine?"

"Just a sec!" boomed the voice that Imogene decided
must belong to Aunt Bobo. "*Jos eee pheen! Jooos eeeeee*

pheeeen! Joooooooooos eeeeeeeeee pheeeeen! You take
those just-washed socks away from your brother's nose."

Imogene cringed. What were her parents thinking?

"Well, what is it?" a voice answered testily.

"Josephine?" asked Imogene.

"Did you hear Bobo call for Josephine and inciden-
tally ruin a good game of stuff-the-socks-up-the-nose just
at the most exciting part?"

"Yes, yes," said Imogene.

"Then who did you expect?" snapped the voice. "All
right. Who is this?"

Imogene was quite taken aback. Was long distance
always this difficult? "It's your cousin Imogene."

"Oh," said Josephine. "Cousin Imogene from New
York. How is New York? How is the Statue of Liberty?"

"Fine, fine."

"I expect you can see it from your window?"

"Well, no, as a matter of fact."

"Then how do you know it's fine? For all you know,
someone might have made off with it. Or the French
might have taken it back in a snit. You know the French.
Right? Hardly responsible behavior for a New Yorker,
is it? We guard our statues here in Iowa more carefully,
let me tell you. And those we don't guard we have the
Chamber of Commerce disguise."

"What?" asked Imogene.

"The Chamber of Commerce hires hundreds of pi-
geons to come every year and sit around disguising the

statues. Though," added Josephine thoughtfully, "at a cost."

"Actually," said Imogene hastily, "it was Iowa I was calling about."

"Oh, yes?" said Josephine, mellowing a bit. "I remember Iowa."

"What do you mean?" said Imogene nervously. "I thought you lived in Iowa."

"I do, of course. Good old Iowa."

"But if you live in Iowa, what do you mean by saying you remember it?"

"Well, of course, if one grows up someplace, one has memories of it, doesn't one? One isn't likely to forget the place where one lives, is one?"

"The thing is," said Imogene, "my mom talked to your mom and they arranged . . ."

"I know," snapped Josephine. "Honestly! Parents!"

"If I decide to come—and it's doubtful," continued Imogene icily, "I'd like to know what Iowa is like."

"Hmmmmmmm." Josephine seemed to give the matter a great deal of thought. "It's a lot like Iowa, and rather like parts of Illinois."

Imogene sighed. "For instance, when you look out your window, what do you see?"

"Well, out of this living-room window I see the Taj Mahal, but out of my bedroom window there's nothing to be seen for miles around but fields of corn and an occasional cow."

"Oh," said Imogene. "What do you *do* all summer, then?"

"The same things we do in the winter," said Josephine. "Only there are more mosquitoes and we teach the new pigs to walk on their hands."

Imogene forgot the reason she had phoned. The thought of pigs walking on their hands had driven it completely from her head.

"It's been keen chatting like this," said Josephine. "But March is throwing potatoes at me." Imogene heard a crash. "You better start running, March. Well, Imogene, I hope you're a good shot with a potato. Toodle-ooo." And Josephine hung up.

Imogene put down the receiver and shut her eyes. It was a nightmare. Socks up her nose, being hit by potatoes, freakish pigs. She knew she would have to go because her parents would never believe any of this. She peeked in on them. They were still chuckling away.

Imogene Bequeaths Her Gum Chain

"**S**o," said Imogene's mother the next morning at breakfast, "in a week you'll be on your way to Iowa. I remember the first time I flew alone. I was quite a bit older than you, and I was flying to college. It was wonderful."

Imogene ate her cereal silently. Only seven more days left until Iowa. Only a week until she would be stampeded by wild pigs and pelted with potatoes.

"Aren't you excited?" chirped her mother, in the way mothers do when they know you are about to do something perfectly dreadful and it's all their fault.

"Excited is the word, all right."

Her mother pursed her lips. "I wish you would try to be a little more cheerful. It was very kind of your Aunt Bobo to invite you to stay with them. You're very lucky to have someplace to go in the summer. There are many children who have to stay in New York." She pressed down the toast lever savagely.

Imogene wasn't in the mood for a lecture. "I think

I'll call Edie Finkelstein," she said, rising from the table and escaping with lightning speed. Edie Finkelstein was Imogene's best friend and understood such things as not caring to spend the summer where the deer and the antelope play. She called Edie to make a date to meet at Rumpelmayer's.

"Rumpelmayer's?" Edie squeaked into the phone. "Who can afford Rumpelmayer's?"

Edie and Imogene often whiled away their Saturdays at Murdock's, where they could nurse a chocolate soda for an hour without spending their whole allowance or being harassed by impatient waitresses. They had only been to Rumpelmayer's once, on the occasion of Edie's birthday, when Mrs. Finkelstein had treated both girls to ice cream in those elegant and rarefied surroundings.

"*I* can afford it," said Imogene. "My father just gave me my summer spending money and, God knows, unless I want to buy a pig, there won't be anything to spend it on."

This statement mystified Edie, but Imogene refused to explain until they met.

On her way to see Edie, Imogene stopped at the drugstore and bought a pair of lime-green sunglasses and a big scarf. She tied the scarf around her pigtails and put on the sunglasses. Now she had the proper mysterious allure. Just right for Rumpelmayer's, and absolutely perfect for intimidating her Iowa cousins.

"*Haha*," she said loudly in a wicked and meaningful way as she approached Edie.

"Haha what?" asked Edie.

"A haha-wrought-of-bitterness haha. I shall keep saying haha all summer, and you would, too, if you had to go where I have to go. Haha," she finished, and walked boldly into Rumpelmayer's.

They were seated in the back at a little cast-iron table. It was a good table for a secret meeting.

"So, what's up?" asked Edie, a trifle unromantically, Imogene felt.

"What's up? What's down? Haha," said Imogene, raising her eyebrows in a most mysterious fashion.

Edie's suspense was building nicely, thought Imogene, when the waitress brought them the menu and they became momentarily sidetracked.

Imogene took out several dollar bills and fanned herself with them languidly as she spoke to the waitress. "We'll have two bowls of chocolate ice cream and coffee."

Edie managed to look nonchalant until the waitress walked away. They always ordered chocolate ice cream. "*Coffee!*" she hissed. "We don't drink coffee. Why did you order coffee? It costs a whole dollar."

Imogene looked bored. "My dear Edie," she intoned lazily, "the last thing we want to do is raise suspicion. Unfortunately, whenever two children dine together without an adult escort, there is bound to be

suspicion as to whether said children will be able to pay the bill. I personally hope they take us for very short, rich grown-ups."

"I think you had better tell me why you have called this meeting," said Edie.

"The time has come, the walrus said, to talk of many things. Of shoes and ships and sealing wax, of cabbages and kings. And why the sea is boiling hot and whether in Iowa pigs have wings," recited Imogene triumphantly.

"Okay," said Edie. "So don't tell me."

"I am not going to camp this summer. I am not making wallets this summer. This summer, I am being sent to stay with my cousins and my aunt and uncle and their pigs and mosquitoes and cows and cornfields and potato fields and probably other dangerous forms of wild-life in, and I hope you appreciate this, Iowa."

Edie digested this information in silence. Imogene was patient. She knew Edie was a little slow, but eventually the seriousness of the situation would sink in. It did. "Ugh," said Edie.

"Indeed," agreed Imogene.

"Ghastly," croaked Edie.

"Precisely," said Imogene.

"How perfectly *stinking*," crescendoed Edie.

"Light dawns," said Imogene, well satisfied.

"What is there to do all summer in Iowa?" asked Edie.

"That is the question," said Imogene. "I doubt I will

last long in the rigors of the wild. My constitution simply can't stand it. It will collapse. But while I am waiting for the collapse to come, I will work on my gum chain. I will work on it from morning to evening, day in and day out. By the time I expire, I will have the longest gum chain in the world."

"Poor thing," said Edie. "Here comes our ice cream."

The waitress placed the ice cream and a pot of coffee in front of the girls. They poured a thimbleful of coffee, the entire cream pitcher, and several teaspoons of sugar in their cups. They sipped this delicacy slowly, each worrying privately that it would stunt her growth.

"Well!" said Edie, spooning ice cream. "I promise to send you my gum wrappers all summer."

"Thank you," said Imogene. "And I will leave my gum chain and my sunglasses to you if I am bitten by a rabid cow."

"Oh, dear," said Edie.

"When are you leaving for Camp Cherokee?" asked Imogene.

Edie and Imogene had always gone to the same camp together, but this year Edie's parents had decided to send her to a camp in Vermont that had a special swimming program.

"Next week," said Edie. "You know, if I hadn't made swim team, I could have gone back to our old camp. I would've had no place to go this summer when it burned down."

"Don't count on it," said Imogene. "Your parents probably have some old relatives in Alaska or something."

"Nah," said Edie. "All my cousins live in New Jersey, and I *like* them."

"Hrumph," snorted Imogene.

The rest of the ice cream was consumed in solemn silence. Imogene stood up smartly, imagining them each shouldering the burden of responsibility. She marched to the cash register to pay the bill.

"Let us walk boldly to our destinies," she said to Edie, preparing to part with her at the door of Rumpelmayer's.

The girls exchanged a dignified handshake.

A Pistachio Woman
and Alligators

The fateful day arrived. Imogene went down to breakfast.

"Good morning, sweetheart," said her father.

"Pancakes for breakfast," said her mother.

The prisoner's last meal, thought Imogene.

"Syrup or jam?" asked Mrs. Spark.

"I *always* take syrup. Always. Already you've forgotten. Boy, I bet there'll be some wild times around here once *I* leave." She picked at her pancakes. True, she ate seven, but she had no appetite for them. "I think I have an incurable disease," she said conversationally.

"No, you haven't, darling. Now go wash your face, or we'll be late."

Imogene glared at her mother, thinking: She thinks she's so smart. "I hope there is a hospital in Iowa," she said as she marched upstairs.

She turned on the steps to repeat her last words

and found her mother right behind her. Imogene put her arms around her mother's neck and hugged her.

"You're going to have an adventure, darling."

Imogene didn't answer, just hugged harder.

"You'll have a wonderful time, and it's only for eight weeks. Eight weeks will fly by."

Imogene wondered why, if this little adventure was to be so wonderful, her mother offered as consolation the thought that it would soon be over. Imogene meant to let go to point this out, but now her mother was hugging her hard. Imogene never wasted a good hug.

It was a quiet ride to the airport. Imogene had a lump in her throat. Her parents checked her baggage and spoke a few words to a flight attendant.

"There," said her mother. "That nice lady is going to take care of you."

Which is more than I can say for you, thought Imogene. But she didn't mean it. Suddenly she wanted her parents to leave quickly. In the waiting area, Mr. Spark developed a tic in his eye. When they called Imogene's flight, he shoved ten dollars in Imogene's pocket and all was bumble and squish until Imogene finally found herself on the plane, sitting by the window next to a large woman who was fumbling with a bag of pistachio nuts and muttering, "It's not possible."

Imogene opened a comic book and tried to look businesslike. The NO SMOKING sign flashed and she buckled her seat belt. "Oh well, I may as well quit anyway," she said to the lady next to her.

The lady turned large, frightened eyes upon her. "Quit what?"

"Smoking. They say it stunts your growth. *Not* that I want to get any taller, particularly. Four foot nine is *quite* enough for me, thank you."

"You smoke?" The woman looked Imogene over. "A little girl like you?"

Imogene decided to change the subject. "Where did you say you were going?"

"Chicago," said the woman. "That's where I'm supposed to be going, but it's not possible. They'll never get a big thing like this off the ground."

"I'm sure you're right," said Imogene soothingly. "But they will make an effort, won't they? Might I have a pistachio nut?"

The woman passed the bag of nuts. "Where are *you* going, little girl?"

At that moment the engines of the plane started rumbling, and without waiting for Imogene's answer, the woman put her head between her knees, assuming the crash position. Imogene considered dropping nutshells down the woman's dress, but thought better of it.

The plane took off and Imogene became too engrossed watching the ground disappear to make conversation. Soon the plane leveled out and soared along. After

a while, Imogene decided that if you'd seen the top of one cloud, you'd seen them all.

"Excuse me," she said, tapping the woman on the neck. "I think you can sit up now."

The woman sat up.

"I see they are planning to feed us while their luck holds out," Imogene said.

The woman looked green. "What are you, some kind of child actor?"

"Heavens, no," said Imogene. "I am the president of a large corporation left to me by my great-grandfather twice removed."

"You can't have a grandfather *removed*," said the lady indignantly. "A grandfather is a direct relative."

"Direct he certainly was," Imogene said, sighing. "Particularly when he was in his cups. That's why they had to keep removing him. But he always came back." Imogene stopped to crack a nut open with her teeth, then continued. "Finally he removed himself." She opened another nut and shifted positions. "One sunny morning, after he'd had his usual breakfast of gin and cornflakes, he became obsessed with the idea that he was a steamroller. He chugged down Fifth Avenue until he fell into an open manhole and was eaten by an alligator, and then I inherited the corporation and I haven't had a moment's peace since."

The woman looked disgusted. "Oh, really?" she be-

gan acidly, when the stewardess arrived with little plas-
ticized meals.

The flight attendant smiled at Imogene and asked
how she was enjoying her flight. Imogene smiled back
and said it was just dandy. She gave Imogene a pair of
pilot's wings to wear on her shirt. Imogene refrained
from telling the stewardess that she was too old for such
nonsense.

"Perhaps you'd like them?" she asked the pistachio
woman after the stewardess had moved on.

"What I'd really like is some peace and quiet," said
the woman. "I never knew a child to tell such elaborate
lies."

"My teacher said I have a fertile imagination." Imogene beamed. "Anyhow, I was only trying to distract
you. I didn't really think you'd believe the part about
the alligator."

"I see." The woman opened her book.

Imogene ate her breakfast and read her comic book,
peeking out the window now and then to make sure the
pilot still had things under control.

The stewardess began collecting the trays. Imogene
looked at her seat companion's untouched tray, eyeing
the blueberry danish. "Be my guest," said the woman,
giving it to her.

"Thanks. This is my second breakfast. Travel makes
me hungry."

"It makes me lose my appetite." The woman sighed. "You must think I'm a terrible coward."

"Oh, no. I was frightened on my first flight, too. Everyone is. Of course, this is nothing compared to flying a two-seater over the Himalayas."

The woman squinted. Then she grinned. "Are you trying to distract me again?"

"Well, maybe." Imogene grinned back.

She looked out the window. Chicago was approaching.

In Chicago, Imogene parted company with the pistachio lady and was hustled to a smaller plane for the flight to Iowa. This time she sat alone and watched the scenery below.

Lordy, lordy, thought Imogene, when they say cornfields, they mean cornfields. She kept a sharp eye out for pigs.

The plane came down, and Imogene looked for her relatives among the crowd of people waiting to meet the passengers. The Reinstein children were not hard to find. They were the contingent standing on their hands.

Josephine Gets the
Last Word

The four fat children remained on their hands. Beside them were two fat adults and a woman so thin she looked like someone had pulled her plug.

Aunt Bobo approached Imogene. "Oh, my," she bellowed. "I'd've knowed you anywhere. You're the spitting image of your mother's sister Marge when she was your age. This is Nathan, March, Annie Mae, and Josephine. Get to your feet, get to your feet, she don't want to shake hands with your toes. And this is your Uncle Bud and your Aunt Emma."

"The family that stands on their hands together demands to be fanned together," said Josephine.

"How is your mother, dear?" asked Aunt Emma.

"Fine, thank you," said Imogene.

Uncle Bud got Imogene's trunk and shepherded them to the pickup truck. The children and Aunt Emma sat in the back, which was a new and exciting experience for Imogene.

The air smelled strange, and March, noticing her

sniff, explained to Imogene that it was pig manure. "You can't do nothing about it. Fact is, I don't smell it anymore, except when it's really bad."

Josephine eyed Imogene quietly as they rattled bumpily along. "I hope," she said at last, "that you had yourself a good look at the Statue of Liberty before you left."

"No," said Imogene.

"It was the least you could do."

"Oh, really?" said Imogene, in what she hoped was a lofty I-am-from-the-city tone.

"For all of us," finished Josephine.

Imogene felt homesick. She looked critically at her summer companions. Annie Mae had a round, pink face with a nose so severely turned up that Imogene caught herself staring up her nostrils. Good grief, she thought, if I were to shine a flashlight up it, I bet I could see her brains. March, the oldest boy, was not as fat as the others. His body was more like an egg than like a rubber ball. He had been kind enough to explain the pig-manure smell. Josephine was impossible. She was the oldest and obviously used to having her own way. Nathan had been so quiet she had scarcely noticed him until he got onto all fours and began to bark.

"Don't mind him," said Aunt Emma in disgust. "He thinks he's a basset hound."

The truck pulled up at a rambling white farmhouse badly in need of a paint job. A big porch circled the front and sides of the house. Creeping vines with purple flowers grew up to the second floor. The screen door in front was broken and flapped gently in the breeze.

Aunt Bobo rolled out of the truck cab. "We thought we'd celebrate your arrival with a picnic dinner," she said. "Josephine, show Imogene around while Aunt Emma and I pack the picnic hamper."

Josephine made a face. "Come on."

Imogene followed Josephine up the stairs, stopping to peek down over the banister into the living room, which had a linoleum floor and a big gas heater in one corner.

"Here's our bedroom," said Josephine, flopping on a bed. "The camp cot over there is yours."

It was a cozy room, with sloping ceilings and windows overlooking the cornfields and barn. There were dotted-swiss curtains and bright Indian blankets on two of the beds.

"Nice," said Imogene politely.

"Yeah, well, we think so," said Josephine challengingly.

"Are you ready, girls?" called Bobo from below.

Annie Mae ran upstairs. "We're taking you for a ride while Pa finishes the chores," she sang out.

"That's nice," said Imogene again. She felt awkward.

"Jos-eeeee-pheeeen!" called Bobo.

The girls ran downstairs and joined the boys in the back of the truck. Aunt Bobo and Emma sat in the cab.

Bobo turned out to be a fearless driver, sending the Iowa dust flying.

"Lots of farms," said Imogene.

"What'd you expect?" asked Josephine.

All the roads looked alike to Imogene. It was hard to make conversation and keep one's balance. They passed a sign: WELCOME TO INFERIOR, population 500, and Bobo slowed down. Aunt Emma slid open the window that separated the cab of the truck from the back, and called to Imogene, "See that blue house? That's where I live." Then the town was gone and Bobo shot off down some more country roads. Finally the Reinstein farm appeared. Uncle Bud came out with the picnic hamper.

"Just got off the phone with your folks, Imogene," he said. "They called to make sure you'd arrived safely."

Imogene thought of her parents and decided to think of something else fast.

They took the basket and began to march through the cornfields. Imogene was feeling sleepy. It had been a long day.

"How's your pa?" asked Bobo. "You know, I never have met him. Come to think of it, your ma hasn't never met Bud either. We need a big family reunion. Gabbing on the phone just ain't the same."

"Uh-huh," said Imogene, thinking: Oh, joy, hundreds of weird relatives mingling over chicken salad.

"Ma says you live in an apartment," Annie Mae said softly, in awe.

"Uh-huh," said Imogene.

"I never been in an apartment," said Annie Mae.

"I have," said Josephine. "You're not missing anything, Annie Mae."

"Josephine, you mind your manners," said Uncle Bud.

Out, out, they continued into the sea of corn. Crickets began to hum, mosquitoes bit Imogene, and the smell of pig manure clung to her. She wished she could step into a bath and go to bed. They marched a long time before they came to a small clearing where a picnic table stood. Corn surrounded them, spreading out endlessly.

"You'll feel more perky after some dinner," said Aunt Bobo as she spread out the sandwiches.

"I made the sandwiches before we left for the airport," said Josephine. "They're my specialty. There's marshmallow and prune, banana and chocolate, cherry jam and cheese, peanut butter for the prosaic, and cream cheese and date."

The children traded sandwich halves companionably, though Josephine insisted on eating all the cherry jam and cheese herself. "Rank has its privileges," she said.

"Oh, Imogene," said Annie Mae, stuffing strawberry pie into her mouth, "I'm so glad you came. We've got such fun planned this summer."

"Of course," said Josephine, "Most of our plans were for four people, but I guess we'll have to make do with five."

"Shut up, Josephine," said March.

It had grown dark. Aunt Bobo, Uncle Bud, and Aunt Emma sat at one corner of the table, talking quietly.

"Come," said March, and he led Imogene and the rest of the children through the corn. He stopped after a few yards and opened a brown package he had taken from the picnic hamper.

"Fireworks!" said Annie Mae and Josephine in glee.

"Bark, bark," said Nathan.

"I got Aunt Emma to pick them up in town today for the celebration. She paid for them out of her secret inheritance."

"Her inheritance?" said Imogene.

"Her *secret* inheritance," said Josephine.

"Some secret, if you know all about it," said Imogene.

"Nobody knows anything about it," squealed Annie Mae, rolling her eyes and, in her excitement, choking on her gum. It took a few minutes to get her to cough it up. Then she proceeded: "It's a deep dark secret and she said she'd tell us about it this summer."

"At some dark and dour hour," said Josephine, getting into the act.

"Bark, bark," said Nathan.

"Nathan," said Josephine sweetly, "everyone knows

dogs, even nice little basset hounds, are never ever allowed to play with fireworks."

Nathan reverted to human form and they split up
the fireworks among them. "Fat but fair" was Imogene's
analysis as they shot the fireworks off into the wide, starry
sky.

The cooling twilight air, full of pig manure, wet
earth, and grassy country smells, the crickets, the large
blue-black sky aflame with bursts of green, yellow, and
red, the muted *ooooo*s and *aaaaaah*s coming from the
picnic table where the grown-ups sat, the sleepy stillness
of summer, all made Imogene feel disoriented. What
was she doing here?

The fireworks ended at last, and the sleepy fat family
plodded home with the cellophany remains of the picnic
in the basket.

Imogene crawled into her camp cot in the room with
Annie Mae and Josephine. Just as delicious sleep was
pulling her down into her pillow, she heard Josephine
mutter, "You'd think she'd have taken at least a peek at
the Statue."

Imogene Swears in Blood

The next morning, Imogene woke up unsure of where she was, the way you always do when you are in a new bed. The sun streamed in the window and the air had the moist warmth of a summer morning threatening to bake to brittle heat. Annie Mae and Josephine were still two doughy lumps under the Indian blankets. Imogene put on her clothes and crept downstairs. Aunt Emma, who frequently popped in before work, and Aunt Bobo sat on the front porch drinking coffee.

"You're up early," said Aunt Bobo. "There's breakfast set out on the kitchen table. Help yourself."

Imogene had filled a plate with eggs and toast just as her cousins slid down the banister.

"Whoa-ho! Whoa-ho!" they cried. "Time to feed the pigs! Whoa-ho!" They dashed out the door. By the time they returned, Imogene had finished her breakfast, Aunt Bobo had gone about her chores, and Aunt Emma had driven off to work.

"Now," said March to Imogene as they convened

on the porch after their breakfast, "today we initiate you into the dread BTWS, the LCCS, and the AGAC."

"These are mysterious and ancient societies," said Josephine. "And I'm not sure you're mysterious enough to belong."

"Shut up, Josephine," said March. "The thing is, today being a warm day, meaning a lake day, we decided to call a meeting of the AGAC. That's the Association of Great Agate Collectors."

"Agates will one day be worth more than diamonds, so, you see, those of us with the foresight to collect them now will one day hold the world's greatest fortune," put in Josephine.

"Here," March continued, taking two small red stones from his pocket. "This is a firestone and this is an agate. Study the difference."

Imogene looked at them.

"We've got a whole box hidden in the barn," squealed Annie Mae.

"But we can't show you where," said Josephine, "until you take the blood oath not to tell anyone of these societies."

"The blood oath?" said Imogene queasily.

"Yes. We take a big knife and we cut your wrist open. That doesn't scare you, does it?" asked Josephine.

"How stupid do you think I am?" said Imogene.

"Don't be a *baby*," said Josephine.

"We do have to prick you with a pin," said March.

"It's not so bad," said Nathan. "It's not like having fleas."

"Forget it," said Imogene.

"You can't have a blood oath without blood!" snapped Josephine. "Oh, wouldn't you know she'd be a Miss Prim and Proper Chicken Liver from New York."

Those were fighting words. Imogene was about to push Josephine off the porch and into the bushes when a prick on her arm arrested her. A mosquito had landed and its stomach was turning red.

"Don't anyone move!" whispered Imogene. She waited until the mosquito had blown up to a good size and then smashed it. "There."

"Oh, Imogene, how clever!" said Annie Mae, and held out a grimy piece of paper with four gray signatures and four little red X's beneath an oath stating that the undersigned would never reveal the secret societies. "Quick, make an X and sign your name."

Imogene made an X with the bloody mosquito and signed her name with the pencil stub Annie Mae offered her.

"Now you're an official member and we can commence the hunt," said March.

A picnic lunch was hastily assembled and they began walking toward the lake, their eyes glued to the gravelly sides of the road. But only Josephine was intent on her purpose. Annie Mae collected more flowers than agates. March heroically offered to carry the picnic basket and

stopped for a little snack now and then. Nathan announced that he smelled a rabbit and ran barking into the fields.

Some society, thought Imogene.

By the time they had turned onto the dirt road that led through the woods to the lake, the sun was beating down and they were dusty and thirsty. It was generally agreed that the search for agates should be abandoned until after the cool refreshment of a swim.

They ran the rest of the way.

There is nothing like being hot and sweaty on a steamy summer day and seeing ahead a wide, clear, blue, sparkling and undulating lake. They sprinted through the water up to their knees and plunged under.

For an hour, all was swimming and diving and playing evolution—a game which Imogene created and everyone, except Josephine, disdained to play.

"First you swim along the bottom of the lake toward the shore," said Imogene, demonstrating to Josephine. "Then you evolve to your hands and knees. Finally you become erect and walk out of the water."

"Better yet," said Josephine, "start as an amoeba." She and Imogene lay motionless and one-celled upon the surface of the lake until March and Nathan chased them with crayfish and evolution evolved into war.

A creek ran into the lake. Josephine and Imogene, who, as amoebas, had become friendly, decided to track it back to its source but soon became discouraged by the marshy muck on both sides of it. They went back to sit in the willow over the lake, where Annie Mae, Nathan, and March were already perched.

The lunch was equitably divided and the children sat companionably, eating sandwiches and picking spiders out of the Kool-Aid. They were finishing lunch, each thinking about the dessert which they had forgotten to pack, when Imogene felt something hit her leg. She looked down and saw a girl throwing stones at her dangling ankles. "Aarg," spluttered Imogene as she almost lost her balance.

"Oh, no," groaned March. "It's snoopy little Sara Anderheimerhooper."

"Good grief," said Josephine *sotto voce* to Imogene. "She lives down the road from us. She and her brothers are our foes to the end."

"Taught your pigs handstands yet? They got nothing on our pigs this year," taunted Sara.

"Really? What are your pigs doing?" asked March craftily.

"Wouldn't you like to know. Who's the kid?"

"The kid," said Imogene, who was developing a distinct aversion to this runny-nosed stone-thrower, "happens to be Imogene Spark from New York City and she was clobbering stone throwers while you were still learning to read. That is, if you have yet."

"Nyah, nyah, nyah," called snoopy little Sara Anderheimerhooper as she went running back toward the road.

"A bright girl," said Imogene. "A remarkable girl."

Josephine heaved a sigh. "Our deadly and murderous foes," she said. "Every year, they enter their pigs in the County Fair annual pig talent show, where pigs perform amazing feats. There's never much competition except between us and the Anderheimerhoopers. Last year they taught their pigs to tap dance, or so they claimed. The pigs had on top hats and they sort of moved around to music, but I don't think you could really call it tap dancing. It's hard to keep finding something new to teach them. We're trying to get our pigs to curtsy this year, but we don't know if the Anderheimerhoopers have come up with something better."

"Why don't we go spy on them?" asked Imogene.

"Impossible," said March. "You can practically see the state line from every window in every Iowa house."

"I have a great deal of natural stealth," argued Imogene.

"Besides, it isn't right to spy on people," said Annie Mae.

"Annie Mae, you listen to me," said Josephine. "Everyone in the entire United States spies on their enemies. It's practically a national pastime. It's practically unpatriotic not to spy on your enemies. The only thing that keeps good U.S. citizens from behaving like beasts is the knowledge that their enemies are spying on them. Without spying, who knows where this country would be."

The children nodded solemnly. Annie Mae turned to Imogene. "She should know. She reads everything."

"Well, what are we waiting for?" said Josephine.

"You forget that it's not that easy," March put in. "There's always someone over there hanging around the barn."

"At night?" asked Josephine knowingly.

The others digested this in silence.

"With a full moon?" added Imogene, who felt that she of natural stealth had better make a few brilliant suggestions herself. "With charcoal on our faces and black clothes?"

"How do we know what the pigs are up to if we visit them at night?" asked March, ever the practical one.

"Well . . ." said Josephine. "We can hum a few bars and waltz around a little to get them into the rehearsal mood and see if they do anything."

The children, exhausted by their own genius, decided that a jump in the lake was needed to cool their hot little brains. All was whales and dolphins until March noticed that the sun was dropping low in the sky and dinner would be ready soon. They scooped up their agates and trotted home.

* * *

After dinner, Imogene crawled out on the roof with
a special-delivery letter from her parents and some sta-
tionery. This was easily accomplished through the bathroom window and was not frowned upon by the adults,
who quite often went out there for their evening coffee.
She settled down and reread:

Dear Imogene,
I'm glad you arrived safely. It's nice to know that you
are now such a capable young lady that Daddy and I can
send you off on planes without having to worry. We miss
your sunshiny face at home.

Her mother went on in this proud-parent vein,
which warmed Imogene's heart despite herself. At the
bottom of the page her father wrote:

Hope all is well and you are having good time. My best
to Bud, Bobo, etc.

Her father was never very chatty in his letters. His
notes always sounded as though he were paying by the
word.

She decided to let her parents off the hook
somewhat.

Dear Mom and Dad,
Iowa is very interesting. I believe I am having the ed-
ucational summer you so devoutly desire for me. It is
true I have always longed for the ocean, but I have
resigned myself to growing up and taking *my* children
there.

Aunt Bobo is a good cook and I haven't come down with any major diseases yet, though I have a spot on my arm that could be the beginning of a rash. Aren't you supposed to watch out for mosquitoes with cholera? And what I want to know is how do you know which mosquitoes are the ones carrying the disease? Oh well.

I hope you are having a nice summer too. I am sleeping under something called an army blanket. Do you know what that is? I miss you too, sometimes. Perhaps you could send me a picture in case I forget what you look like. Just kidding. Haha.

Love,
Imogene

Then she wrote to Edie Finkelstein.

Dear Edie,
I trust you are now up to your armpits in wallets and pining for a little news. Iowa certainly delivers all the corn and pigs it promises. I am embroiled in secret espionage plots which are too secret even to tell my best friend. I am also a blood member of a secret society. I guess my talent for natural stealth was bound to be discovered. Perhaps one day you too will be invited to join a secret society. It is best to get yourself a large kerchief and a pair of dark glasses to be on the safe side.

I miss you and home but good grief let's not get too emotional.

Write soon.
Your friend,
Imogene Spark

She folded up her letters and put them in pink envelopes and went into the house. Aunt Bobo came upstairs to say good night.

"The moon's getting orange," she said as she tucked them in. "It won't be too long before we have a midsummer moon."

"What's a midsummer moon?" asked Imogene.

"Once a summer," said Bobo, "the moon rises full and orange like a harvest moon. We got to calling it the midsummer moon."

Josephine and Imogene looked at each other across the room and smiled.

A Tactical Error

After days of sun and swimming, Imogene awoke to a thunderstorm. She watched the rain pitch furiously against the corn.

"Darn, no lake today," she said, and woke Josephine by jumping up and down on her bed. Josephine, in sleepy self-defense, pushed Imogene onto Annie Mae's bed. Annie Mae awoke with a squeal and threw the alarm clock out the window (the reason for which she was somewhat at odds to explain later). The alarm clock hit March on the shoulder as he was on his way to feed the pigs, and March, seeing Nathan emerge from the door, assumed he was the culprit. By breakfast, no one was speaking to anyone else.

After breakfast, Imogene went moodily up to the attic to find her trunk. She took some gum wrappers out of it and began folding them. Josephine came up after a while with a book. "Oh, *you're* here," she said, before settling down to read.

"Rain, rain, rain. Endless rain. It never rains in New York," said Imogene as she folded wrappers.

"Pig manure," said Josephine. "What's that you're doing?"

"I'm making the longest gum chain in the world."

"A likely story."

"It's rolled up in my trunk." Imogene opened her trunk to display the tightly rolled ball of the gigantic gum chain. It was almost three feet in diameter.

"*Wow!*" said Josephine. "You chew all that gum?"

"Of course not. I'd have to chew for years and years without a break to get all those wrappers. No," said Imogene. "I have seventy-two people saving gum wrappers for me. Some of them I don't even know. Someday I am going to send this to *The Guinness Book of World Records* and then I am going to go on talk shows, have my picture on the cover of *Time* magazine, and retire to a desert island, where I will refuse interviews."

"I don't know about the desert-island part, but I bet that could get into *The Guinness Book of World Records*. Can you show me how to do it?"

"Nobody works on this chain but me. It has to be the longest chain by one person."

"Glory hog," said Josephine, and picked up her book. She put her book down. "I'm bored. Let's find the others and have a meeting of the LCCS and BTWS."

Josephine left to hunt up March and Nathan and Annie Mae, who were skulking around the house.

"Does this mean another blood oath?" asked Imogene when they were all gathered in the attic.

"Naw," said March. "The LCCS is the Laundry Chute Climbing Society, and the BTWS is the Bathtub Walking Society."

"We've been expressly forbidden to climb the laundry chute because the adults are sure we'll fall down the chute or get stuck," put in Josephine.

"But no one's caught us at bathtub walking yet," said March.

They went into the upstairs bathroom, in which sat an enormous, old-fashioned bathtub, the kind perched on porcelain clawed feet. The children showed Imogene how to walk along its wide rim as though tightrope walking. When one reached the opposite side of the tub, the title of Bathtub Walker Level One was awarded. Then it became trickier. Level Two involved walking sideways; Level Three, walking backwards; Level Four, hopping on one foot. So far, as Annie Mae explained, no one had made it to Level Four. The children pursued this reckless and daring game for an hour. Imogene had just made it to Level Three when lunch was called.

Aunt Bobo announced over chicken noodle soup and peanut-butter-and-jelly sandwiches that she was going into the nearby town of Inferior to pick up groceries and Aunt Emma, who was coming over for dinner. Aunt Emma worked as a checker in the Bunny Food Grocery Store. The children were invited along. Allowances were

pooled, with Imogene contributing an equal amount out
of her summer spending money. It was found that they
had enough for a truly disgusting debauch of penny
candy—so they hopped into the back of the pickup truck
and headed for town.

Even in the rain, the town was an exciting diversion
from cornfields. Inferior consisted of a small variety
store, two saloons, two gas stations which were rivals to
the death, the Bunny Food Grocery Store, a hardware
store, and a drugstore with a lovely, glaring orange
REXALL sign beckoning the children to the delights of a
soda fountain and penny-candy counter. For ten minutes
the children argued whether they should split up the
money and each get a bag of penny candy or blow the
whole sum on a large hot fudge, marshmallow, and
cherry delight sundae with five spoons. In the heat of
the argument, March tried to stick an old piece of string
in Josephine's left ear. Josephine told Annie Mae she
was adopted. March told Annie Mae she wasn't. Nathan
claimed he wanted to buy dog biscuits.

Imogene ignored them all. Her attention was
riveted on where the penny candy was kept, behind a
three-tiered glass counter, away from greedy, dirty little
fingers. When the children decided on penny candy, the
girl who tended the soda fountain placed the desired
tidbits in little brown bags as they made their agonizing
choices. There were malt balls, licorice sticks, licorice

shoestrings in red or black, jawbreakers of all colors, bubble gum in several guises, candy cigarettes, candy lipstick, chocolate wafers coated in sparkles, taffy, cellophane containers of chocolate balls, Lik-m-aid, and a score of other exotic delights.

After they had driven the counter girl into a state of despair, the children took their purchases and went for a walk along the main and only drag. They tried, as always, to peer into the frosted windows of the saloons to see what kind of degenerates were inside at one in the afternoon. As always, someone came by and scolded them for hanging around a saloon.

"What would your mothers say?" asked Mrs. Ferguson, an unpleasantly plump woman in a powder-blue pants suit.

"Wouldn't you feel terrible," suggested Josephine, "if it turned out we were orphans?"

"I was sired by a basset hound, myself," said Nathan.

"Of all the naughty things to say!" sniffed Mrs. Ferguson.

"Oh, no," said March. "He really believes it. You mustn't mind him."

"Bark, bark," said Nathan.

"I shall report you to . . . to . . ." Mrs. Ferguson faltered.

"The SPCA?" asked Josephine sweetly.

"Certainly not," snapped Mrs. Ferguson. "You are

badly bred children, that is quite clear. Liars, all of you. Telling me that Nathan thinks he's a dog!" And she shifted her purchases to her other hip and trotted down the road.

"A smart woman." Imogene giggled.

"Probably a member of Mensa," agreed Josephine.

"Oh, dear," said Annie Mae, who thought even interfering fat ladies in powder-blue pants suits should be dealt with kindly. She was going to run after her and apologize, when along came the pickup truck with Bobo and Aunt Emma.

The children hopped in. As they passed Mrs. Ferguson, Aunt Emma called back through the open truck window, "There's Loulou. I just heard that she's going to judge the pig talent show this year. They announced it at the town meeting we missed last week. Stop, Bobo, and let's give her a lift."

The children's blood ran as icy rivers.

"Don't. Oh, please, don't," said March.

"Why ever not?" asked Aunt Emma. "The poor woman has another ten blocks to walk, and it looks like more rain. That shiftless husband of hers has undoubtedly taken the car and gone into town to look for the seedier side of life. Bobo, pull over."

Imogene would have liked to ask what the seedier side of life was, but now was not the time. "The poor woman needs the exercise. Anyone can see that," she said hopefully.

"Probably looked forward to this walk all day long," agreed March.

"Who are we to spoil a pleasant day's outing with our nasty truck?" Josephine chimed in.

Aunt Emma cast a gimlet eye in their direction. "Terrorizing the locals again," she grunted. "Drive on, Bobo."

Aunt Bobo pursed her lips. "I hear the Anderheimerhooper children baked Loulou a chocolate cake. Nice kids, them Anderheimerhoopers. Hearts in the right places. Good set of pigs this year, too."

"The sneaks," whispered March.

"This is great, just great," Josephine hissed as the children leaned closer to her so the grown-ups wouldn't hear. "They've never announced a judge this early. Now what do we do?"

"We could bake her *two* chocolate cakes," said Imogene weakly.

"We could bake her chocolate cakes until we dropped dead from exhaustion, and do you think she would accept them from four ill-bred children and a dodo who thinks he's a basset hound?" said Josephine.

"Then what?" asked March.

"We could prey upon her sympathies," said Annie Mae, repeating a phrase her teacher frequently used.

"She probably doesn't have any," said March. Josephine and Imogene agreed.

"She must have *some* kindly sympathies," insisted

Annie Mae, "or she wouldn't have said anything about children hanging around a saloon."

"Oh, that was just snoopiness," said March. "The town's full of it."

"We could save her husband from the seedier side of life," suggested Imogene doubtfully. "Then she'd have to be grateful to us forever."

All eyes turned to Imogene. Four hands thumped her proudly on the back.

"Eureka! That's it," said Josephine.

"There's just one problem," said March. "Does anyone here know what the seedier side of life is?"

"I think it's the foul depths to which the human spirit can sink," whispered Imogene.

"Now what the hell does that mean?" shouted Josephine, forgetting to whisper.

"Josephine!" said Bobo.

"The murky oblivion of the soul," hissed Imogene, ignoring Josephine's rudeness.

"Oh, crap!" screamed Josephine.

"Josephine!" snapped Bobo. "You watch your mouth, or before you know it, it's going to be full of soap."

"I'll murky oblivion you," whispered Josephine. "I think you talk like that just to pretend you're better than us."

"That's how you always talk, Josephine," said

March. "Like somebody from one of those books you're always reading, or something."

"I do not," said Josephine.

"She does, doesn't she?" March asked Annie Mae.

"Well, sometimes," said Annie Mae fairly.

"I wouldn't be caught dead talking like that," said Josephine. "You don't know *what* the seedier side of life is."

"I may not know specifically," admitted Imogene, "but I know it's worse than wiping your nose on your sleeve."

"*That* much we could have figured out," said Josephine scathingly.

"We could ask," said Nathan.

"Grown-ups never tell you that type of thing," said Josephine.

"Well, then," said Imogene, undaunted, "we will have to go on a quest."

That night, Imogene wrote another letter to Edie Finkelstein.

Dear Edie,

Why haven't you written me yet? This is already my second letter to you. Do you have to spend every spare minute in the water at this swimming camp of yours? If I were you, I would come up for air once in a while. In fact, I would skip swim period to go write my best friend a letter. But you are not as adventurous as me so I guess you're stuck there swimming back and forth all summer. You have my sympathy, old pal.

Your friend,

Imogene Spark

P.S. My cousin Josephine is almost as adventurous as me.

P.P.S. How about that for a surprise?

P.P.P.S. I miss you anyway.

Midsummer Moon over
Mr. Ferguson

What with toads to catch and a crayfish aquarium to build, it was several days before the children got back to the quest. When they did, they met on the roof to discuss it.

"As I see it," said Josephine, "the important thing is to determine what Loulou's husband is up to."

The others concurred.

"I think we should follow him," continued Josephine.

"Beard him in his lair," put in Imogene.

"Right," said March. "But this is going to be hard if we don't know when he's home."

"We'll probably find him home if we go early enough," said Josephine.

"Or *late* enough," said Imogene, who still liked the idea of midnight sleuthing.

"Early is better, I think," said March. "Then we can follow him all day."

"That means we're already too late," said Annie Mae.

"Ten o'clock and no rabbits caught," agreed Nathan.

There was a disappointed silence.

"Pooh," said Imogene.

"Don't pooh so fast there," said Josephine. "Have you forgotten what tonight is?"

The others stared at her blankly.

"The midsummer moon, you cretins," said Josephine in exasperation. "Stealth by night into the enemy camp and pigs to spy upon."

"Do you mean spy on the pigs all night and Mr. Ferguson at dawn? Won't we get awfully tired?" asked March doubtfully.

"Nonsense," said Josephine. "We'll take naps this afternoon and prime our pockets with cookies for the long night vigil. We'll become nighthawks, nocturnal creatures, the secret order of owls."

"Dogs can see in the dark." No one paid Nathan any attention.

"Stay out all night?" said Imogene, who had never done this before. "Oh boy, oh boy, oh boy."

"Naps," scoffed March. "Naps are for toddlers."

"Not this kind of nap, you lunkhead." Josephine glared at him. "Am I forever to be the sole creative thinker around here? Can you only think of your own paltry ego? These naps are secret. The kind enemy agents take before they go on deeds of derring-do."

Imogene, who was a bit miffed about being left out of the creative-thinker category, said, "Knights go on deeds of derring-do. Secret agents go on missions."

Josephine waved this away.

"Well, anyway," said March, "I don't think I can nap in the middle of the day."

"Hmmmmmm," said Josephine. "You may have a point. We'll have to think of sleepiness techniques. The question is, what makes one sleepy?"

The children thought.

"Church," said Imogene.

"Long rabbit chases," said Nathan.

"Uncle Edward," said Annie Mae and was immediately sorry. Uncle Edward was an old bore who visited once a year from Texas.

"Sunday dinner," said March.

"Country air," said Imogene, and the others frowned at her.

"What else is there around here but country air?" Josephine wanted to know. "What are you telling us? That we go around in a perpetual fog?"

Edie Finkelstein would understand, thought Imogene.

"Come on," said Josephine. "We have to do better than this."

"Lots of swimming," said Annie Mae.

"*Gooooot*. Verrrrry goot," said Josephine.

"Rabies," said Nathan.

"Oh, *will* you shut up while I think?" said Josephine.

"*Milk!*" screamed Imogene. "*Milk milk milk milk milk milk milk milk*. That's what they always give you at night when they want you to sleep. Warm milk."

"Bingo," said March.

"Hoopla," said Josephine. "That and swimming. Lots of swimming and then lying in the sun with milk to drink. If that doesn't do it, nothing will."

They climbed back in the bathroom window, slid down the banister, and went into the kitchen, where Aunt Bobo was making cinnamon rolls.

"You must have smelled the rolls," she said.

"No time for rolls," said Josephine as she got a big jug of milk out of the refrigerator and started to leave the kitchen.

"Wait one minute there," said Aunt Bobo. "Where are you going with that milk?"

"We're going on a picnic," said March.

"With just milk?" asked Bobo.

"That's right. National Drink More Calcium Week. Milk is the order of the day. Yum yum, milk," said Josephine.

"I don't know what you're up to, but at least it's healthy. You better pour that milk into a thermos if you're going far. It's too hot to leave it out for long," said Bobo.

"But the thermos isn't *big* enough. We need a *lot*

of milk," said Josephine, pretending to faint out of sheer exasperation.

Aunt Bobo, who knew this for the slimy tactic it was, ignored it.

"I guess we'll have to drink it here," said March.

"Fizzlesticks!" screamed Josephine, coming back to life. She sat down with the other children. They drank glass after glass—a somewhat bilious chore—the monotony relieved here and there by a cinnamon roll. When they finished, they announced, "To the lake."

"Absolutely no swimming until your food settles," said Aunt Bobo.

"You sure are being difficult today," said Josephine.

"That may be as that may be."

The children gave her a collective withering look and marched off to the lake.

They plopped down by the shore.

"Well, perhaps just lying in the sun with all this milk in our stomachs will do it," said Annie Mae, ever optimistic.

The children lay in the grass and stared out at the enticingly sparkling lake. The sun was high in the sky and it was warm on the ground. A breeze moved over the top of the grass, causing it to bend and tickle the children, whose stomachs were contentedly digesting cinnamon rolls and milk. Insects buzzed industriously in the background. The next thing they knew, the sun was over on the other side of the lake.

Imogene woke first and ran into the lake. Her splashes woke the others, who soon joined her. They took a short swim, deciding it was best to save their energy for the long night vigil.

They ran home, and parted, to pursue their separate, quiet activities. Josephine read her library books. She was happily making her way through everything Louisa May Alcott wrote. Nathan buried bones in the back yard. Imogene worked on her gum chain. March wrote letters to his congressman, something he had learned to do in school last year. As the afternoon wore on, he began to run out of legitimate complaints and took to writing about his last visit to the dentist. Annie Mae washed her dolls' clothes amid a storm of derisive remarks from Josephine, who scorned this type of futile domesticity.

Finally, it was dinnertime. The children sat around the dinner table, twitching.

"Lands," said Aunt Bobo. "You'd think you'd been set on by a pack of mosquitoes. Must be the midsummer moon."

"Midsummer moon," agreed Uncle Bud. "Who's up for a midnight dip and some fishing out on the lake?"

This was the ultimate of summer charms: fishing at night, with a midsummer moon *and* a midnight dip (though seldom taken at midnight). But tonight the children almost groaned. Would these grown-ups never stop meddling? The children flashed looks across the table, in the silent understanding that to be less than enthusiastic would almost certainly arouse suspicions.

"Oh, boy," said March.

"Nifty keen," said Nathan, forgetting to bark.

"Wowee zowee," said Imogene.

"Well then, grab yer poles and let's go dig some bait," said Uncle Bud.

The children's annoyance couldn't last long, for worm digging has its own charms. So had the rickety old rowboat that they rowed out into the still black lake. Then the moon rose. Imogene had never seen anything so big and orange in her life. The moon she knew was small and white, but this was enormous. It was stupendous. It glowed with a vaporish yellow light. As it rose, the moon grew smaller, fading to pale gold. Then they fished.

The moon left a wide path of light on the lake, which Uncle Bud rowed into and along as he looked for a better fishing spot. He saw another boat out in the distance.

"Looks like Duke has caught something. He can always pick the spots, the old so-and-so."

They put the anchor down. The man in the other boat reeled in a good-sized fish. Bud chuckled.

"Whatcha got there, Ferguson?" he called across the water.

The children almost fell out of the boat.

"Is that Loulou's husband over there?" asked Josephine, straining to get a good look at the man's face.

"Yep. Best fisherman in the state," said Bud. "Practically cleans out the lake every season."

"Holy cow," said March. "Let's row over and see what he's up to."

"He's fishing. Bait your hooks," Bud said.

Josephine leaned over to Imogene and whispered, "So close and yet so far. How do we know he's *really* fishing?"

Imogene nodded. It was simply too dark, even by moonlight, to get a good look at the man.

"Well, maybe we can go when he's done fishing and take a look at what he caught," Josephine said.

"Maybe. Now let's try to get something of our own," said her father.

They fished in silence. Imogene caught a small rock bass that had to be thrown back, and Nathan caught a good-sized perch. Everyone waited excitedly for another tug on a line. After a while, Uncle Bud said, "Well, I guess you folks must be getting sleepy. How about a quick dip and then we'll go?"

"But we didn't get to check on Mr. Ferguson. I mean, his fish," said Annie Mae.

Uncle Bud gave a long-suffering sigh and started to row over to Mr. Ferguson's boat.

"Hey, Duke," he called. "You mind showing these kids what you caught? I won't never get them to bed otherwise."

Mr. Ferguson turned silently toward them, a large,

dark man. Annie Mae cowered in the corner of their boat, and even Josephine felt a little tense as Mr. Ferguson lifted his catch up out of the water for the children to see.

"Quite a catch, isn't it, kids?" said Uncle Bud.

"Uh-huh," said Josephine, who, like the others, was vastly disappointed to find Mr. Ferguson had been fishing after all.

"We got us a perch or two," said Uncle Bud. "But I don't think they're really biting tonight. Least not where we were."

Mr. Ferguson shook his head. He was obviously a man of few words. Uncle Bud rowed back to shore.

The children took their clothes off on the shore and stood shivering in their swimsuits. When they plunged in, they found the water warmer than the air. Imogene thought the dark, warm waves almost magical. They swam underwater and looked up at the singe on the lake. A singe, as the children explained to Imogene, was the path of light the moon made on the water. A burn was the path of light the sun made. Imogene thought this was useful and esoteric information and she stored it to tell Edie Finkelstein. Then the group headed home. The children had to appear innocent as they took their baths and went through the ritual of being tucked into bed. When the silence of the house signaled sleeping adults, they would dress and meet on the front porch. Imogene, waiting for the silence, wondered how she could feel sleepy after the nap she had taken that day. A gentle snore issued from Annie Mae.

"Don't worry," whispered Josephine. "We'll wake her up when the coast is clear."

They heard the muted voices of Bud and Bobo from downstairs. As always, Imogene wondered what adults talked about together when they were alone at the end of the day. Did they save up all the tidbits they couldn't tell their children? Whatever could these tidbits be? The air was crisp. She felt pleasantly waterlogged, wind-blown, and mosquito bitten. The faintly musty smell of the old army blanket wrapped about her agreeably.

Then it was morning.

In the Chute

Imogene opened her eyes to a gray early-morning light. The cornfields were wet with dew. She checked Annie Mae's clock. Rats! Four-thirty.

"Get up, get up, get up. What happened?" she whispered to Annie Mae and Josephine.

"What do you mean?" asked Josephine crabbily, and then realized what time it was. "Why didn't you wake me up?" she shrieked.

"We all fell asleep," said Imogene glumly.

"The boys, too?" asked Josephine. They rushed to the boys' room, where they were sound asleep. To atone for thinking the boys had gone on alone, they woke them up with a minimum of cold water.

"Why didn't you wake us at midnight?" asked March angrily.

"We *all* fell asleep," Josephine answered coldly.

"Get dressed quick," said Imogene, hopping around on her cold bare feet. "Hurry, hurry, hurry. All is not lost. We can still follow Mr. Ferguson."

The children threw on their clothes, wasting little time in remorse for lost pig-sleuthing. They ran down the stairs, not even stopping for some early-morning sustenance, so great was their haste. At the barn they stopped dead.

"Oh," said Annie Mae.

"Gosh," said March. "Gee."

"*What?*" screamed Imogene.

"Bark, bark."

"Let's *move* it," screamed Imogene.

"That's just the problem," said March. "The thing is, we've only got four bikes."

Imogene digested this in silence. Should she selflessly demand that they go off on the quest without her? She, whose idea it had been? She could always stay here and work on her gum chain, and there were letters to Edie Finkelstein to be written.

The others waited. Nathan was almost cowering beside the barn. Imogene opened her mouth, fully intending to tell the Reinsteins to ride forth on their trusty steeds without her, but all that came out was "*Arrrrrrrrrrrgh.*"

Josephine snapped to attention. "Argh nothing," she said. "She can take the horse."

The Reinsteins had an old horse named Clarence who had spent the last few years of his life walking the farm, being a horse, which was all the Reinsteins had in mind when they bought him.

"That horse has never done a lick of work in his life," said Josephine. "And he can jolly well be of some use for a change."

"A heroine on a horse." Imogene rather liked the idea.

"Ummmmm," said March, toying with his shoelaces. "Uh, if we follow Mr. Ferguson, you know, in stealth and all that, I mean, we can always ditch the bicycles to hide in the bushes and stuff, but, that is, a horse is not going to be so easy to ditch."

"Go!" said Imogene. "Go on. Get moving. *I* have important business correspondence to keep up with, anyway." She stalked into the house and up the stairs and got her gum chain. In the attic, she sat folding wrappers and thinking: They're so fat their bikes will probably collapse. What can you expect from people in Iowa? This led her to think about New York and what her mother and father would be doing at this moment. Probably sitting in the kitchen, getting ready to go to work. Probably having forgotten all about her. Their friends would say to them, "And how is Imogene?" and they would reply, "Imogene who?" And while she wasn't *really* crying, a tear or two dimmed her eyes, until a clump, clump, clump was heard on the stairs and in burst Josephine.

"*Well,*" she said loudly, clumping rapidly around the room in circles. "Well, well, well, well, well. Of course, someone has to do the tedious sleuthing today,

but naturally, being lunkheads, that is to say, having a
lot of natural lunk, they completely forgot that this is the
day we always climb the laundry chute. It is time for a
meeting of the LCCS. *They* can sleuth and report to us
tonight. After all, the groundwork, which is purely routine, is always done by the plebes in any society. It is
the brains at the top that wait in their offices, or, in this
case, their laundry chutes, for the reports and casualties
to come in. Come on, I'll be chief commander and you
can be my secretary."

Imogene was touched by this show of loyalty. So
touched she actually let Josephine fold a few gum wrappers, although not quite touched enough to accept being
designated secretary. A small argument ensued as to
whether an organization could have two chiefs. Josephine
finally allowed that it might be possible. "But sloppy,"
she said. "A sloppy way to run an organization."

Imogene and Josephine ran downstairs to eat breakfast, and left a note for Bobo saying they had all gone on
a long, long bicycle ride. Then they went to the cellar,
where the laundry chute ended. The laundry chute was
a wooden tunnel that went straight up through the four
flights of the house. It was just wide enough for a child
to shinny up if she pressed her sneakered feet against
the sides of it. The children had climbed it regularly
before the practice was banned by the adults. It was an
arduous climb, but one could stop at the various floors
and eavesdrop. Usually, all one heard was Bobo making

beds and singing an aria from *Aida*, but occasionally something of interest came to the children's ears, like the time Mrs. Anderheimerhooper had asked to borrow the phone on the third floor.

Josephine had knocked lightly on the laundry-chute door, then shinnied up above it, where in the deep dark recesses she couldn't be seen. Sure enough, Mrs. Anderheimerhooper excused herself to her husband, who was on the other end of the line, and opened the laundry-chute door. She peered down. She peered up. She could see nothing. "This is most peculiar, Henry," Josephine heard her say into the phone. "I could have sworn . . ." And Josephine climbed down and knocked again. This time Mrs. Anderheimerhooper flew to the door, but again Josephine was well out of sight. Josephine couldn't hear what good old Henry was saying, but Mrs. Anderheimerhooper declared into the phone, "It is *not* my diet." Mrs. Anderheimerhooper prided herself on keeping her girlish figure and would eat nothing but watermelon pickles for days, or would go on a diet where she could eat all the food she liked but only with a clothespin on her nose so she couldn't taste it. "This whole house is crazy, and I'm sorry Bill Tyler ever sold it to these people. I am coming home now, and if I hear one more word about my diet, I am going to wash your colored shirts in with the white clothes. So I am, Henry Anderheimerhooper, one word and I'm warning you, there won't be a single white sheet in the house *and* I shall leave the nuts out of my banana bread!" And she hung up.

"I shall leave the nuts out of my banana bread" became an inside joke among the children, and they often threatened each other and their parents with it when exasperated.

Josephine explained all this to Imogene as she taught her the rudiments of climbing. It was trickier than it looked. "Almost like being a human fly," said Imogene, working up a sweat and beginning to think this sport wildly overrated. She was not about to give up, however, not when she had a sneaking suspicion that it might put her in the position of secretary to the chief commander. She finally made it to the second-floor landing and decided to rest. It was a bit cramped, but, I, Imogene Spark, she thought, have been in tighter situations than this.

A foot grazed her head. "Ouch, watch it," said Imogene. "Now what?"

"Now we sit and wait for something to happen on this floor."

They sat and waited. Downstairs, Bobo and Bud were having breakfast, but the girls couldn't hear their conversation. Then came the sound of people going upstairs. "And how's Pearl?" they heard Bobo ask. Someone said Pearl was just fine.

"That must be the vet, Dr. Cooper. Daddy wanted him to look at one of the cows. This is great. Ma will give him some coffee in the upstairs parlor and we'll hear every word."

Imogene couldn't imagine anything interesting issuing forth from the mouth of a vet with a wife named Pearl.

"You're up and about early," said Bobo. "Bud wasn't expecting you until this afternoon."

"The Anderheimerhoopers had an emergency with two of their pigs, and seeing as how I was out this way, I thought I would kill two birds with one stone. I guess a vet oughta say 'cure two birds with one stone.' Ha ha ha. Gotta be careful what I say, I'm seein' Miss Havary later."

"Is her canary sick?" asked Bobo.

"Bird's fine. Miss Havary oughta get herself a hobby and stop making up diseases for that bird to get. Hiya, Bud," said Dr. Cooper as the girls heard a third person come into the room.

"Harvey, how are you? You say there's something wrong with the Anderheimerhooper pigs?" asked Bud.

"Scraped nose and, I suspect, a stress fracture," said Dr. Cooper.

"You don't say?" said Bud. "Now how'd you suppose that happened? I don't suppose it had nothin' to do with their stunt for the pig talent contest?"

"That's just what I *do* think," said Dr. Cooper. "They got those pigs in little soccer shirts and kid-sized tennis shoes, pushing a ball around with their snouts."

"Trying to teach them to play soccer, are they?" asked Bud.

"Now, Bud," said Bobo, "the pig talent contest is the kids' responsibility and you and me had best stay out of it. I got enough trouble keeping the peace with Cora as it is."

"All right," agreed Bud. "I'll be in the barn, Harvey."

"Just want to finish my coffee, Bud," said Dr. Cooper. "You're smart to stay out of this, Bobo. You folks don't overwork your pigs, I'm glad to say, but half the county has their pigs rehearsing from dawn until dusk. That's probably why so many of them lose interest and quit before the contest. Maybe I'm getting too old for this job. Don't have the patience I once did for this nonsense. Tennis shoes, did you ever?"

"Have another cup of coffee," said Bobo.

"Nope, better go down and have a look at that cow. I suppose you got her in toe shoes. Har har har," he chuckled, recovering his good humor, and they heard the two descend the stairs.

"Pssst," said Josephine. "Did you hear that? What a scoop. The Anderheimerhoopers are teaching their pigs to play soccer."

Josephine was so excited that she lost her footing and landed on Imogene, who lost her footing, and the two of them fell all the way to the piles of laundry at the bottom of the laundry chute with a loud thump. Before

they could disentangle themselves, Aunt Bobo was standing over them.

"How many times have I told you . . ." began the well-worn lecture. It ended with the two of them prisoners in their bedroom for the rest of the day, but even this failed to dampen the spirits of the girls. They spent the rest of the afternoon waiting for the other agents to come home and folding gum wrappers, which Imogene allowed Josephine to do as long as she, Imogene, was the one who actually made the chain.

Under the Bushes

The three spies with bicycles waited breathlessly in the bushes of the Fergusons' back yard. As nothing happened, breathless turned to stoic and, alas, to crabby.

"Where *are* they?" muttered March irritably.

"Maybe this is just their mailing address," said Annie Mae, who had heard of such things.

"Maybe he murdered Loulou and chopped her into pieces and buried her in the basement," said March, who wasn't ready to give up hope that they were onto something big.

"Oh, no!" squealed Annie Mae.

"I don't care," said Nathan, whose stomach was rumbling. "I'm hungry. I wish I'd stayed home with Josephine."

This was the way with Nathan. He was either a basset hound or a baby. March sighed in exasperation. He was hungry, too. Having left without breakfast now seemed like the height of folly.

"Nathan, I have an assignment for you," said March

wearily. "Can you get to the Bunny Food Grocery Store in Inferior by yourself?"

"Yes," said Nathan.

"Good. Then your job is to go hit Aunt Emma for a loan. Tell her we'll pay her back out of our allowances. Get some donuts and chocolate milk and bring it back here. But be *careful*. Leave your bike back where we hid ours, and if someone is around, don't come near the bushes."

"I wanna go, too!" said Annie Mae. "I'm getting cold and it's wet under these bushes and I'm afraid Nathan will get lost."

March frowned. He was beginning to understand how it was to be the oldest.

"Okay," he said. "You can go, too, but don't blame me if you get back and I'm off sleuthing. You'll only have your stomachs to blame."

Nathan and Annie Mae rode off. Ten minutes is a long ride into town when you haven't had breakfast. By the time they had leaned their bikes against the Bunny Food Grocery Store, they were ravenous. Inside, Aunt Emma stood behind the counter talking to a customer. The children waited patiently for the woman to leave and then approached Aunt Emma.

"Men, men, men," Aunt Emma muttered to herself. Aunt Emma muttered this often. She had gone through four husbands. "That poor woman. That poor, poor woman. Her husband has taken up roller skating. Not satisfied with skating alone, he thinks *she* should join him. Honest to Bejesus. And why roller skating? Because in the midst of his last hobby, which was reading *New York* magazine, he had come across an article that said roller skating had become the craze in New York. Well, everyone knows that New Yorkers are a wild bunch. I'm not surprised by anything they do, least of all tying wheels to their feet and rolling along with the traffic, but you'd expect a nice middle-aged Iowa man to have better sense. 'Ethel,' I said to her, 'you ought to have known it when you married him and already he had a stack of *Gourmet* magazines hidden in the closet. You can't trust a man like that. Whimsical. Pining for the good life, whatever that is. Not that you can trust any man when he reaches a certain age. Whatever they're missing, they're not going to find it in *New York*.' "

"Can we borrow a couple of dollars?" said the children.

Aunt Emma came out of her reverie reluctantly and looked at them. "What are you kids doing in town so early?"

"Just biked in, but we need breakfast money."

"Why don't you bike on home for breakfast? Why didn't you pack something? Where are Imogene, Josephine, and March?"

Aunt Emma was a sharp cookie. The children realized they had a snow job ahead of them.

"Well," said Annie Mae, who was in a quandary

because she didn't want to lie. "It's kind of a secret mission we're on and we didn't have enough bikes for everyone so March and Nathan and I came in alone and then we found out our mission would take up more time than we thought and we haven't eaten and our allowances are all used up for this week."

"Think ahead," said Aunt Emma. "Next time, *think ahead*." But she gave them five dollars and also a package of day-old danish.

Annie Mae spent fifty cents on chocolate milk and then, with four-fifty left, had a brilliant idea.

"Listen, Nathan," she said, a little uncertainly, "We're supposed to be spies, aren't we?"

"Yes," said Nathan. He was trying hard not to open the danish.

"So we ought to have a disguise, oughtn't we?"

"Sure, I guess. Annie Mae, can I have some danish now?"

"No, it wouldn't be fair. We have to wait for March."

"I thought you'd say that," Nathan said glumly.

"Let's go to the drugstore," said Annie Mae. "I want to see if they have something."

"Penny candy!" shouted Nathan.

"No, no, a disguise, Nathan dear," she said, and put her arm around his shoulder. She liked to hug Nathan when the others weren't around.

They rode over to the drugstore. There, by the hairnets, was a whole box of plastic sunglasses, just like the ones Imogene kept on her dresser. Sitting on top of the pile was a hot-pink pair. Annie Mae knew she was meant to have them. She bought a yellow pair for Nathan and a turquoise pair for March.

They rode back, stashed the bikes, and crept quietly into the yard. March was still under the bushes.

"What took you so long?" he asked.

"Here," she said, offering him the first drink from the chocolate-milk carton. He was better-tempered after that. She gave him the turquoise sunglasses, saying, "I thought we ought to have a disguise."

"Good thinking," March began, when the door opened and out came Loulou.

She put a tablecloth on the iron lawn table and began to set it with coffee cups. A long white car pulled up and a large woman in a yellow-and-lime-green pants suit emerged.

"Myrtle!" cried Loulou. "Coffee's almost perked. Sit down. My, don't you look lovely."

"New perm," said Myrtle, patting her hair. "Did you make these scrumptious donuts, Loulou? Shame on you. You know I have to watch my weight."

"Nonsense," said Loulou. "I was just saying to the girls at the meeting for the Beautification of the Dump that I'd love to be as trim as you." She wiped a tear from her eye.

"My poor dear," said Myrtle. "What on earth is the matter?"

"I'll just get the coffee. Then we'll have a good confab," said Loulou, and shuffled off to the kitchen.

Myrtle went around the side of the house, calling, "I'll just have a peek at your roses, dear. Mine are doing so badly this year."

The three children had been up for hours. The chocolate milk and day-old danish had merely whetted their appetites.

March whispered, "Gosh, are they going to eat *all* those donuts?"

Annie Mae said, "They *did* say they had to watch their weight."

Creeping to the table, March grabbed three and ran back under the bushes, where he split them among the three of them. They giggled.

Myrtle came back and sat down at the table. Loulou brought out the coffee. Even though the donuts seemed to be arranged in a random pile, Loulou knew that now there were only nine. She smirked at Myrtle.

"My, my, you do like donuts, don't you?" she tittered.

"Oh, I do, dear," said Myrtle. "But I'm afraid I just can't eat any today. My diet, you know. Just a little black coffee for me."

Loulou regarded her skeptically and poured the coffee.

"Where's Duke?" asked Myrtle. "Gone to town?"

"At this hour?" asked Loulou in disgust. "He doesn't

stir until noon anymore." And she began to cry gently into her coffee.

"Oh, my dear, he's not ill, is he?" asked Myrtle.

"Ill?" choked Loulou. "I should say not. I almost wish he was when I think on the likely alternatives. He sneaks out at night after he comes home from fishing. Goes out after I've gone to bed and doesn't come back for hours. What am I going to do? I never thought this could happen to me."

"Tsk, tsk," said Myrtle with relish. "How long has this been going on?"

"Let's see," said Loulou, blowing her nose. "Must have started the same night I was voted judge of the pig talent contest."

Myrtle nodded sagely.

"But what can I *do*?" Loulou erupted into sobs again.

"Wait it out. Now go in and wash your face and I'll get my tatting from the car. There's nothing like a new tatting pattern to keep your mind off your troubles." Myrtle put an arm on Loulou's shoulder and led her to the house.

"Aren't they going to eat those donuts?" asked Annie Mae.

"Waste not, want not," said March, already crawling toward the table. He took another three.

Loulou came back to the table with her face washed. Myrtle returned shortly after with her knitting bag. This time *she* noticed that half the donuts were missing.

"I don't want to offend you, dear," Myrtle said gently, "but donuts never solved anything. Half a dozen donuts in one morning is a little excessive."

Loulou's face turned bright red. "Me! You milk cow. You know very well *you* ate those donuts."

Myrtle stood up. "Milk cow?! I didn't eat one, you elephant."

"Oh, no," said Loulou sarcastically. "It wasn't me. It wasn't you. No doubt there are pixies hiding in the bushes."

The ladies were standing up, hands on hips, scowling at each other. The children began to giggle. They tried to muffle it, but the more they tried, the closer they came to an explosion. Annie Mae looked at March, who was desperately holding both hands over his mouth. They gave up and roared, pounding the ground, wiggling. Luckily, Nathan looked up in time to see the ladies descending on them. He jabbed March and Annie Mae, and the three of them ran lickety-split down the road, grabbing their bikes.

Aunt Emma came to the house that night. In a burst of romance such as parents are sometimes subject to, Mr. Reinstein had offered to take Mrs. Reinstein all the way into Taterville. It was exciting just to watch Bobo, in her good black dress, high heels, and pearls, stand in front of the mirror and put on her lipstick and perfume. At times like this, Josephine thought her mother became

a different person. Her voice, when she spoke to the children, was honeyed and calm. "You look just like a movie star," said Annie Mae, and Bobo laughed, a gentle, tinkling laugh. She kissed all the children good night and then sailed off with Bud, who looked quite the man-about-town himself in a tie and jacket.

When they had gone, Aunt Emma settled down to fixing dinner. Aunt Emma's husbands, it had been rumored, had left her in self-defense, several dinners and lunches after their wedding. She was a creative cook. Tonight she was putting together a casserole of tuna fish, noodles, lima beans, and some leftover mozzarella she found in the fridge.

"And now," she said as she settled herself at the table, "I have a rather interesting story to tell you children. It seems that Mrs. Ferguson was visited by three juvenile delinquents who stole six jelly donuts and caused her and Miss Myrtle Hassenfeffer grief enough that they retired to dark rooms for the rest of the day to nurse sick headaches. No clue to the children's identity was found except an empty box of day-old danish from the Bunny Food Grocery Store and an empty chocolate-milk carton. Loulou says she couldn't tell who they were, as they wore dark glasses."

"I told you that was a good disguise," whispered Annie Mae to March.

"Shhh," said March.

"Ahem!" Aunt Emma continued. "Juvenile delinquency is said to be running rampant, but I never thought I'd live to see it here in Inferior."

The children picked at their casserole.

"Oh, all right," said Josephine in disgust. "That was us, but the situation was completely misunderstood. The plan was to save Mr. Ferguson from the seedier side of life and therefore put Loulou Ferguson forever in our debt. Since no one around here told us what they meant by the seedier side of life"—here she gave Aunt Emma a long, accusing look—"we were forced to become spies. Our intentions were good. Now let us drop this unpleasant subject and return to this perfectly delectable dinner."

Aunt Emma's mouth was grim, but her eyes were not. "I see," she said. "The intentions sound more self-serving than noble to me, and, frankly, more than a little half-witted. The way to win this contest is still to come up with the most talented pigs, and I haven't noticed you concentrating too hard on that. You don't have much rehearsal time left."

"We were trying to teach them to curtsy, but we can't get them to bend their knees properly," said March.

"Hmmmm," said Aunt Emma. "That's not a bad stunt. Not at all. What you need is some professional coaching. I'll get Miss Betula Beefay from Inferior to come in. She runs a dancing school. I always help her make the recital costumes, so I'm sure she'd be glad to assist. Next week we'll begin serious pig rehearsals. Now stop sulking and let's have a game of hearts."

The wind picked up and a storm set in. It was a wonderfully terrifying summer storm, with thunder ripping the lid off the sky. The rain poured down steadily, making a calming, swishing noise in the background. To make things perfect, the lights went out and the children had to play cards by candlelight.

All of a sudden, a plop was heard and then a frantic scratching noise.

"Man the ice tongs!" screeched Josephine. Imogene looked down to where the children were bent over a large black beetle. "Happens whenever it rains," said Josephine. The beetles had their own little hole in the wall, from which they would fall and start a mad scramble across the floor. The children took turns catching them with the ice tongs and flushing them down the toilet. They were a pack of heartless beetle hunters.

When Aunt Emma claimed she couldn't play one more hand of hearts, they all went out to the porch and watched the lightning flash across the cornfields.

I am a lone pioneer woman, thought Imogene, huddled in an old wicker rocker. They sat and rocked well past the children's bedtime.

"I always like to eat maple-nut ice cream during a storm, myself," Aunt Emma said, and went inside to get some. Imogene followed, and the two of them brought out the ice cream and bowls. Annie Mae and Nathan had fallen asleep, so March and Aunt Emma and Josephine and Imogene ate ice cream in the roaring wind until two headlights appeared in the black distance and Aunt Emma sat up with a start.

"Oh, good Moses," she said. "I think I was supposed to put you to bed. Yes, it seems to me now that that's why I was here to begin with."

"We'll never tell," said Josephine, climbing the stairs sleepily.

"I bet you won't," said Aunt Emma. "Now remember, serious rehearsals next week. We'll give those Anderheimerhoopers a run for their money."

An Unexpected Pleasure

The next week, as the children lay basking by the side of the lake in the late-afternoon sun, Josephine sat up suddenly. "The AGAC has been sadly neglected," she said. So they dried off and walked down the road, looking for agates.

Glancing up for a second, Imogene saw a dim figure coming toward them, lugging a knapsack. She stared. "Aaahh!" she cried.

The others gathered around her quickly, looking down at her feet.

"It can't be!" Imogene gasped.

"Where? Where?" Josephine squatted in front of her, sifting the gravel for the agate she thought Imogene had spotted.

Imogene pointed down the road. Josephine looked up to where she was pointing.

"You're *supposed* to be looking for agates," she said to Imogene.

"That's *Edie*!" screamed Imogene. "That's Edie Finkelstein!" And she went galloping toward the figure. The other children stood in the road, watching.

"*Edie!*" screamed Imogene when she reached her. "What are you *doing* here?"

"Hello, Imogene," said Edie, rather inadequately, Imogene thought.

"How did you *get* here?"

"I took the bus," said Edie, and then sat down on the side of the road. She brushed her blunt-cut dark hair out of her face and wiped her enormous square-framed glasses on her shirt. "It was a long trip, Imogene, you have no idea. You *flew.*"

Edie often exasperated Imogene, but this had knocked the words right out of her.

"I'm starving," Edie added mildly.

"This won't do, Edie," said Imogene. "This really won't do. Showing up in Iowa and then saying things like you took the bus and you're starving. You're not telling me *anything.*"

"Anyhow, now you have to admit that I'm adventurous," said Edie.

"What?" screamed Imogene.

"Admit it," insisted Edie.

"What are you talking about?" demanded Imogene.

"In your letter you said you and Josephine were adventurous but I wasn't. I guess I proved you wrong, huh?"

"Edie," said Imogene, beginning to get nervous,

"you don't come all the way across America because someone suggests you *might* not be the adventurous sort. How did you do it?"

"It was all Laura Beth's idea," said Edie.

"And *who* is Laura Beth?" asked Imogene.

"She had the bottom bunk. I had the top. Anyhow, between swim periods we were making a lot of wallets as usual, and so she thought, why not sell them? We used to go during free-activity hour and sell them on the road. Then my uncle sent me some money to buy the whole cabin banana splits. Laura Beth and I got a kick out of that. She chipped in some money her grandmother sent her. Her grandmother sends her ten dollars a week. Can you believe that, Imogene?"

"Forget Laura Beth's grandmother!"

"Laura Beth thought it would be neat if I just showed up here. After the counselor said good night, Laura Beth put pillows in my bunk so it looked like I was there. I walked to the Greyhound station and got a bus to Iowa. I left a note saying I was going on a little vacation and would be back sometime later and to tell my parents not to worry. Anyhow, I told Laura Beth she could spill the beans if they tortured her, but otherwise to keep quiet for a few days. It was much easier than you'd think. I should have done it a long time ago. So here I am."

"Well," said Imogene. "Well. And just where are we supposed to hide you? Or did you think Bud and

Bobo wouldn't happen to notice another head at dinner? Good grief, Edie, you haven't thought this out at all. Your parents have probably called the police. And if we keep this a secret, I will get in as much trouble as you, and Lord knows, you're probably grounded for life as it is."

"Actually, I have that all worked out. When your parents ask why you were harboring a criminal, just tell them that I never told you my parents didn't know where I was. Say that I lied to you. I can't get in any worse trouble than I am already."

"This is most unlike you," said Imogene. She introduced Edie to her cousins, who were impressed with Edie's adventure. However, they agreed that hiding Edie was going to pose a problem.

"The only grown-up who is apt to take our side is Aunt Emma," said Josephine. "Let's go see what she suggests."

So the children turned around and headed to Inferior and the Bunny Food Grocery Store. It was a long, hot, dusty walk, and they were all very hungry by the time they got to the store, where Aunt Emma had just gotten off work. She invited them for supper. Josephine phoned home from the store to get Bobo's permission. Then they drove to Aunt Emma's.

Aunt Emma's house was a periwinkle-blue cottage surrounded on four sides by great Douglas pines. Hollyhocks, tiger lilies, pansies, forget-me-nots, daisies, black-eyed susans, and irises grew wherever they had taken a fancy to sprout. Inside was a lot of ancient, battered furniture and some old wicker pieces painted in vivid shades of rose. The children explained Edie's plight to Aunt Emma as she bustled about, making a casserole of chicken and potatoes and cream of asparagus soup.

"Well, I hate to disappoint you," said Aunt Emma when the story was finished, "but we are going to have to telephone Mr. and Mrs. Finkelstein. Now."

In consideration of Edie's finer feelings, the children tiptoed out to sit on the front porch as Edie morosely dialed home. Half an hour later, she and Aunt Emma appeared on the porch, carrying dinner.

"How did it go?" asked Imogene.

"They were pretty mad," said Edie. "Your Aunt Emma said I could stay here with her for the rest of the summer. They wouldn't let me do that, but I can stay a week, and they are sending me return airfare home."

Edie Finkelstein was her best friend, but Imogene was glad that she would be leaving in a week. It is often this way when you have two sets of friends who get together and you are in the middle. "Tough luck, kid," she said, and attacked her casserole with gusto.

Aunt Emma saw Edie flinch at Imogene's remark. "I'll tell you what," she said briskly. "Since Edie will only be here a week, I'll take you all into Taterville on my day off. We'll spend the day in town and go to dinner and a movie at night. Where would you like to go?"

Of course, the children said Matty's, a restaurant that served seventy-two kinds of hamburgers. The Reinsteins were so delighted that they slapped Edie on the back and promised to make her an honorary member of the BTWS. Imogene thought Edie was eliciting an unwarranted amount of praise, but was mollified when she found that Edie's knapsack was full of gum wrappers she and her cabin mates had been saving.

After the dishes were done, they hopped into Aunt Emma's car and went to pick up Miss Betula Beefay. Miss Beefay was tall and bony, with folds of skin hanging around her neck like a chicken, and wiry orange hair. The children found her fascinating.

"I haven't never taught pigs to curtsy," Miss Beefay said as they drove to the Reinsteins', "but when your Aunt Emma called, I said to myself, why not? A good teacher can teach anybody. I even suggested to Clark Gable that he learn how to dance. It just might advance your career, I said. He didn't say nothing back. You know a lot of them movie stars are real shy at heart. But let your light so shine, they tell us, let your light so shine."

Edie looked frightened. Imogene would have been frightened a month ago, but now she felt right at home. She and Josephine looked at each other and smothered giggles behind their hands.

The pigs were dozing quietly when the children came into the barn, but leapt up when Miss Betula entered calling, *"And a five, six, seven, eight!"* After putting the pigs through a rigorous audition to see which ones could bend their knees, Miss Beefay gathered the pigs in a circle around her.

"Okay, my fat darlings," she said to them. "It's showtime. There's only a few weeks until the contest, and the act's a mess. Now, which one of you fellers has got the rudiments of a curtsy down pat?"

The pigs just looked at her sullenly, the way pigs that are not eating do.

"Heavens to Betsy. Not a trooper in the bunch," said Miss Beefay to Aunt Emma.

"Well," said Josephine, who was really very fond of her pigs, "you have to coax them a bit. Pigs aren't natural performers, you know."

"Nonsense," said Miss Beefay. "Why do you think they call show-offs 'hams'? I hate to tell you, kiddo, but what you got yourself is a bunch of real dumb pigs."

"They are not," protested March. "Let me show you." He tapped gently on the pig's back, which was the signal for it to curtsy. After several taps, the pig bent its front knee, lost interest, and strolled outside. "Well, it's a start," said March defensively.

Miss Beefay ran her hands through her orange hair and paced. "Let me think this through. Let me think this out," she said, pacing with increased agitation. The others waited patiently.

"What's she upset about?" whispered Josephine to Imogene. "I thought that pig did okay."

"She's not really despairing. That's artistic temperament," whispered Imogene back. "You see a lot of it in New York."

"Shhh," said Miss Beefay. She paced some more. "I've got it. You know, in show biz we entice our performers to greatness with unions. You wanna be in the union, you gotta put out. Now how do you explain unions to a pig?"

"I don't know," began Aunt Emma. "I think you gotta remember, Betula, you are dealing here with small-brained mammals . . ."

But she was overruled by the children, who thought it was a wonderful and novel idea. They split up and began chasing the pigs around, whispering in their ears about a union called pig equity. Then they gathered the pigs together and Miss Beefay called, *"And a five, six, seven, eight, curtsy!"*

The pigs went out and rolled in the mud.

"Pigs got no pride," said Miss Beefay sadly. "That was my trump card."

March jumped forward. "No, you were *right*, Miss Beefay. It was a brilliant idea."

"How so?" asked Miss Beefay, patting her hair uncertainly.

"We have to entice the pigs with a reward, but pigs have no pride," March continued. "All a pig thinks about is its next meal. If we entice a pig to curtsy, it will have

to be with food. Something sugary, I think. Pigs love little sugary treats."

"That was my next suggestion," said Miss Beefay. "Or it would have been if I knew anything about pigs, which I don't, of course, having spent my days in more refined company. By all means, let's entice these pigs with sugary treats."

Annie Mae ran into the house. Bobo gave her a box of sugar cubes, and the children, under the direction of Miss Beefay, taught the pigs to bend their knees, rewarding each good curtsy with a sugar cube. Sure enough, the pigs began to catch on.

By eight-thirty, everyone was exhausted. They retired to the porch to drink lemonade with Bud and Bobo and watch the stars come out. Bobo had gotten a phone call from Imogene's parents. They hadn't known about Edie, so Mr. and Mrs. Spark asked that Imogene call them when she got in. She did this now, explaining that she had had no part in Edie's impulsive decision to come to Iowa.

"It sounds rather like one of your ideas, dear," said her mother.

"I must be rubbing off on Edie," agreed Imogene.

When Imogene hung up, she found Edie had fallen asleep on the porch. Aunt Emma carried Edie to the car. Miss Beefay hopped in the back and they drove off.

"We seem to be attracting adventure this summer," whispered Josephine later as they undressed for bed beside a snoring Annie Mae, "even on our off-days. We haven't even had a good game of stuff-the-socks-up-the-nose. Busy, busy, busy."

"Are we really going to make Edie a member of the BTWS?"

"Honorary member," said Josephine. "It's not the same. It's like an honorary degree. You know, you give it to someone whether they know anything or not. That's what Aunt Emma said, anyway. It means absolutely turkey necks as far as I'm concerned."

"Speaking of turkey necks," said Imogene, "how do you like Miss Betula Beefay?" And the girls lapsed into such gales of giggles that they had to stand on their heads on the bed with their feet against the wall to stop. Then Imogene plopped back into bed, singing herself a little ditty of la-di-da-oh-roke-dee-doe, and fell asleep with a warm feeling in her stomach.

For the next few days, Aunt Emma drove Edie over in the morning and took her home after pig rehearsals. The children alternated between rehearsing the pigs, which they had to do for two hours each morning and evening, and showing Edie the ropes. They took her to the lake and played evolution, showed her how the BTWS worked, and even dragged out the big box of agates. Edie seemed duly impressed with it all. "Your summers, at least, have important and meaningful pursuits," she said, sighing. "It makes swimming laps and making wallets look even more futile, and that's not easy, believe you me."

Friday rolled around quickly. The children dressed in their best going-to-Taterville clothes.

Aunt Emma picked them up after breakfast and they drove the forty miles of cornfields singing songs in what Aunt Emma called seven-part disharmony.

At Woolworth's, the children spent a blissful hour shopping. Josephine and Edie each bought a pair of sunglasses so that now everyone had a pair. Then came a boring hour trailing at Aunt Emma's heels as she did her grown-up errands, which seemed to consist of buying an endless supply of underwear. One of the errands was at the large department store, which boasted three escalators. Escalators were old hat to Edie and Imogene, but the Reinstein children rode up and down fourteen times before they could be dragged away. Lunch was at the local ice-cream parlor, where Aunt Emma, who was not health-minded, let the children order anything they wanted. She had a chicken sandwich and a cup of tea. The children, exalting in their freedom, ordered banana splits, sundaes, sodas, and strawberry shortcake. Then they went to a movie. *The Sound of Music* and *Dracula Meets the Wolfman* were both playing in town. March and Nathan wanted to see *Dracula Meets the Wolfman*, but they were overruled. The movie was a big-screen, Technicolor, popcorn-munching treat, and the children sat spellbound. Afterwards, walking dizzily up the aisle with jujubes stuck between their teeth, Josephine, Edie, and Imogene decided they were going to become nuns.

At Matty's, the children looked around at the other tables to see if anyone had ordered the dessert burger, a hamburger with chocolate ice cream, but no one had. They made their selections, vowing that *next* time they would try some of the more exotic burgers.

After dinner, they had a quiet stroll about town. Rounding a corner, they ran smack into the whole herd of Anderheimerhoopers.

"Well, well, well," said Aunt Emma. "How are you, Cora? Henry?" The adults stood about, chatting, as the children moved off to another corner to heap abuse upon each other.

"*We* get to see a movie," said snoopy little Sara Anderheimerhooper.

"We saw *The Sound of Music*," said Annie Mae.

"That's a *baby* movie," said Junior Anderheimerhooper.

"Oh, yeah?" said Josephine. "You've got bananas where your brains should be."

"Your *pigs* have bananas where their brains should be," said Horace Anderheimerhooper. "Wait until the show this year. Our pigs are gonna walk away with the prizes."

"Your pigs are just pushing around a dumb old soccer ball," said Edie. "The Reinstein pigs are getting professional coaching."

The Reinsteins and Imogene turned to Edie in horror. How could she? The *last*, the very *last* thing they wanted was to let the Anderheimerhoopers know they were on to them.

Aunt Emma pulled the children away at that most alarming of moments, as Mr. and Mrs. Anderheimerhooper went into the movie, followed by their stunned children.

"Anderheimerhooper reprisals will be forthcoming," said Josephine as they drove back to the farm. "Oh boy, oh boy, I know you didn't know any better, Edie, but you sure did mess this up."

Edie was almost in tears.

"Now, now," said Aunt Emma. "What can they actually do, after all?"

The children thought. The list was long.

A Heated Afternoon

The next morning, the children went with Aunt Emma to drive Edie to the airport. Edie seemed a little nervous, but whether due to the plane trip or to anticipation of wrathful parents, Imogene couldn't tell. She pressed on Edie several small agates and a bouquet of forget-me-nots.

"Farewell, oh faithful friend," said Imogene.

"See you in a few," said Edie glumly, and walked that long and lonely road to the boarding area, with the Reinstein children waving behind her.

Josephine brushed an imaginary piece of lint off her shirt. "Well, that's that," she said briskly.

They drove home in silence. The day had turned hot and muggy. After lunch they sat on the roof, cooling their feet in a basin of cold water, sipping lemonade, and keeping an eye on the barn, where they expected the Anderheimerhoopers to show up.

"I wish we could go to the lake," whined Annie Mae.

Everyone thought of the enticingly clear and cool waters, and more than one expressed a desire to shove Annie Mae's head into the threshing machine.

"I don't see why we all have to stand guard over the barn," she persisted.

"Well," said Josephine, "I suppose we could go in shifts, but two, at least, should remain on the roof, in case the sneaky Anderheimerhoopers show up. I'll stay if someone stays with me."

Imogene offered to, and the rest gave a whoop and ran off.

Imogene got her gum chain and started to fold wrappers languidly.

"Here, I'll help you," said Josephine, beginning to reach for the gum wrappers. "Just sitting here is boring."

"Sorry," said Imogene. "But it has to be the longest chain by one person."

"Big deal," said Josephine. "Who's going to know if I link a few wrappers?"

"I'll know," said Imogene primly.

Josephine glared. "I'll tell you something else," she said, raising her voice. "No one is ever going to *care*, because *The Guinness Book of World Records* is never going to be interested in your stupid chain."

Imogene put her chain down, and her eyes filled with tears, but she scrunched them up so Josephine couldn't see. "Oh, yeah? Well, who cares about a bunch of stupid pigs? Oink, oink, oink. Typical of you Iowa hicks."

"I knew it!" screamed Josephine, getting to her feet. "Big-city know-it-all. At least we *shared* our pigs. Big-city snob."

"Oink, oink, oink."

"Selfish. Dog-in-the-manger."

"Oinkety oink, oink, oink."

Josephine picked up the lemonade pitcher and threw its contents at Imogene. It splashed on her gum chain.

"Look what you did!" cried Imogene, aghast.

Just then Bobo stuck her head out the bathroom window. "What's going on here?" she asked.

The girls stared at each other in stony silence.

"I hope you're not fighting," said Bobo. "Who threw that lemonade all over the roof?"

"Josephine," said Imogene.

"Tattletale," said Josephine.

"Josephine, you remember you're Imogene's host," said Bobo.

"Grrrr," said Josephine.

"And clean up that sticky mess before it attracts flies," Bobo said, and went back to her housework.

"Yeah, clean it up," said Imogene, and, taking her gum chain, went back inside. She spent the rest of the afternoon sitting in the attic, hating Iowa. She was de-

spising farms in particular, when she heard March and
Nathan and Annie Mae scramble out on the roof.

"Okay," she heard March say. "You guys can go
now."

"I wouldn't go to a cat fight with that traitor," said
Josephine.

"Where's Imogene?" asked Annie Mae.

"Who cares?" said Josephine.

"But she's your best friend," said Annie Mae.

"Used to be my best friend," said Josephine. "Now
she is a slime bucket."

"Oh, brother, " said March. "Why don't you go find
her and make up?"

"Why don't you stick a bean up your nose?" coun-
tered Josephine, and stormed into the house. She took
a book and went out into the cornfields to brood.

Dinner was uncomfortable.

"Boiling up for a storm," said Bobo.

"Have you ever noticed how Iowa has the best
storms?" said Josephine.

"New York has storms," said Imogene.

No one said much after that.

After dinner, Imogene said she had a stomachache
and was going to lie down. When the others had gone
to the barn, she crawled out on the roof and peeked at
them. Miss Beefay and Aunt Emma were already with
the pigs.

"I'll just go say hello to her," she heard Aunt Emma

say after the rehearsal. She dashed back to her bed and
tried to look wan.

"Hi," said Aunt Emma, sticking her head through
the door. "I bet it's the heat that's making you feel so
poorly. Why don't you come to the lake and cool off?"

"Okay," Imogene said weakly. She followed Aunt
Emma down to her car. Miss Beefay was sitting in the
front seat and Josephine was sitting in the back seat. She
made a face when she saw Imogene. The other children
had gone up to the roof to watch the barn.

"I didn't know I was your best friend," Imogene
hissed as Aunt Emma pulled out of the driveway.

"Were," Josephine hissed back.

"You never told *me*," said Imogene accusingly.

"I thought it was understood," said Josephine. "Oh
well, it doesn't make any difference now."

In the front seat, Miss Beefay and Aunt Emma were
deep in conversation.

"You know," said Imogene slowly, "the part of my
gum chain that got splashed with lemonade has to be
remade. I sure could use some help."

"Why don't you get Edie to help you? She's *your*
best friend, isn't she?"

Aunt Emma parked the car by the willow. Josephine
hopped out and ran into the lake. Imogene followed her.

"You can have two best friends, you know," she said,
swimming up to Josephine.

Josephine dove under and emerged spitting water

through her teeth. "I hate it when it gets this hot. It turns me into a beast."

Imogene spun in circles in the water. "I have been a beastlier beast," she said happily.

"Yes, you have," said Josephine.

"I have not," said Imogene.

"Enough of this," said Josephine. She giggled. "I called Annie Mae and Nathan witless rabbits when we were rehearsing the pigs. They kept forgetting to tap the pigs on their backs. Oh well, I guess Annie Mae is still pretty young."

"And Nathan is only a puppy," said Imogene, and the girls giggled, spitting water gleefully at each other.

"We better head back," called Aunt Emma from the shore.

The girls dried off and they drove home, where everyone had already gone to bed. Imogene and Josephine climbed onto the roof to feel the cool evening breezes. They could hear the low rumbling of thunder in the west, coming closer and closer. They were flapping their elbows, pretending to be chickens, when they heard a sound. Josephine clutched Imogene's elbow.

"There's someone down by the barn!"

The Dark and Dour Hour

"The pigs!" screamed the girls, and tore for the barn, where, over the wind and falling rain, they heard pigs making high-pitched, horrible squeals as they stampeded out into the cornfields. An albino chipmunk streaked by the barn door.

"An albino chipmunk!" shrieked Josephine. *"Who put an albino chipmunk in here?"*

Out in the cornfields, the Anderheimerhoopers, scared out of their wits by the unexpected success of their plan, were trying to recapture the pigs on stampede. When they saw Josephine and Imogene, they ran for home.

The rest of the Reinsteins burst out of the house. "Holy Mother Maud," cried Bobo. "What has happened? What has happened?" And she ran helter-skelter across the cornfields in her bathrobe.

"We've got to round them up," said Bud. "Circle the cornfields."

"Oh, mercy," cried Bobo as she ran after a pig.

Josephine and Imogene went after a large sow who had leaped into a mud puddle. They collided, slipping in the mud, and the sow squealed as Josephine fell on top of it. "Grab her leg!" screamed Imogene, who was lying on her stomach in the mud. Josephine grabbed the sow around the ankle. "Those Anderheimerhoopers have gone too far," she choked, spitting out mud.

The girls led the sow back to the barn, where they met Annie Mae, dripping wet and sniffling, leading another pig back to its stall. Then they dashed back to the fields.

The rest of the night was a blur of movement, wind, and rain. When the last pig was safely locked in, the Reinsteins took quick baths, and Bobo, looking grim, gathered up their muddy pajamas to put in the laundry.

"I'll call the vet in the morning," said Bud wearily, and everyone went back to bed.

Josephine sat on her bed and stared out the window.

"What's the matter?" asked Imogene finally.

"Just look at the corn," said Josephine in a stricken voice.

Imogene went over to the window. Great patches of corn lay bent and flattened where it had been broken in the scuffle.

"Oh, no," Imogene said softly. She put her arm around Josephine.

* * *

By the time the children got up, the vet had already seen the pigs.

"Well, it's finally gotten out of hand," he said, stamping mud off his boots.

"How are they?" asked Bobo.

"Oh, nothing serious. A few scrapes and contusions. You're lucky it's no worse. But God Almighty," he said, his face reddening, "I knew this was gonna happen someday, Bobo. Everyone's taking this gol-dern talent contest too seriously. You know what them crazy Wallabees up in the north part of the county did? They were nosing around my office asking about steroids. They heard that some athletes inject themselves with steroids. They were gonna inject their *pigs* with the jeazly stuff and train them to lift barbells. I'm going to go have a word with Cora and let her know what kind of pranks those little angels of hers are up to these days. This whole thing could escalate until someone's pigs really are injured. Sorry about your corn," he added.

"Come have a cup of coffee," Bobo said, sighing, and they disappeared into the kitchen.

The children sneaked out to the barn to see for themselves that the pigs were all right. March idly tapped one of the pigs. The pig snorted and turned around. "Oh, no," said March.

"Come on," said Josephine. "Leave him alone. Let's go back to the house."

March tapped again. "Oh, no," he muttered.

"What's the matter with you?" barked Josephine. "Leave the poor thing alone."

"Don't you get it?" asked March. "This was our most talented pig. He was the pride of Miss Beefay. He always bent his knees when I tapped."

"Maybe he's just tired," said Josephine. "Try another."

In a panic, the children gently tapped pig after pig. The pigs didn't respond.

"It's the shock," said Josephine finally. "They've forgotten everything."

"It's all over," said March, and went back to the house. The other children tripped dispiritedly upstairs after him.

March collapsed face down on his bed.

Josephine put a pillow over her head. "I can't believe this," came her muffled moan.

"Let's discuss this calmly," said Imogene.

"Bark, bark," said Nathan.

"Why don't we go to the attic and work on my gum chain and figure things out?"

"I don't know how to make a gum chain," said Annie Mae.

"Come on, I'll teach you," said Imogene, pulling her off the floor. The others followed.

Imogene taught them how to rip and fold wrappers. As they worked, they tried to think of something they could teach the pigs in the little time remaining.

By suppertime, the gum chain had grown amazingly, but they were in despair over the pigs.

Bobo called them down for dinner. Aunt Emma had come with sympathy and a cherry pie. "I heard," she said.

The children nodded glumly.

"You might as well tell Miss Beefay to stay home," said March. "We'll never retrain the pigs in time."

"Since when did you kids turn into quitters?" asked Aunt Emma as they brought their pie out to the porch. "Heck, if I had been a quitter, I never would have found my fortune."

"Your fortune?" said Josephine, perking up for the first time all day.

"But I don't suppose you want to hear that old story? Could I trouble you for some coffee, Bobo?" said Aunt Emma.

"You promised," said Josephine. "You promised you'd tell us at some dark and dour hour. The hour will never be darker."

"Ah, but is it dour?" asked Aunt Emma.

"The dourest," said March, who had no idea what dour was.

"I did promise. Well, it was when I was in between husbands. I think it was between Harry and Phil, but it might have been between Phil and Leopold."

"Yes, yes," said Josephine.

"In between, anyway. I had just moved into my cottage, the one I have now. It was covered with this awful black-and-gold wallpaper. You remember that wallpaper, Bobo?"

Bobo handed Aunt Emma her coffee. "I sure do. Jeez, that was dingy stuff. Gold tulips, wasn't it?"

"Cabbage roses," corrected Aunt Emma.

"*Anyway*," said Josephine.

"Anyway," Aunt Emma went on, "I was stripping the stuff off, when behind a corner of the wallpaper in the bedroom I found a piece of yellowed old parchment. I was about to throw it out when I noticed that it had funny markings. Holding it under the light, I saw it was a map of the garden. I wondered why a map of the garden was behind the bedroom wallpaper. Then I noticed an X over one of the rosebushes."

"A treasure map!" squealed Annie Mae.

"That's exactly what I thought. Sixty years ago, the house had been owned by a cantankerous old miser named Willy Snoot. Folks said he was rich, but he died without a family or a will, and no one ever found any of his money. Maybe he didn't have any."

"Or maybe he buried it in the garden," said March.

"Exactly," agreed Aunt Emma. "I grabbed a shovel and went out to the rosebush and dug it right up. I dug one foot, I dug two feet, and guess what I found?"

"Treasure!" cried the children.

"Nothing. Not a blessed thing. I sure felt silly. I went back to fixing up the house. I was lying in bed that night when it occurred to me that perhaps I had the map upside down and had been digging under *the wrong rosebush*. I hopped out of that bed and headed for the garden like a bat out of hell. There I was, in my night-gown, digging away under the other rosebush. One foot, two feet, and lo and behold . . ."

"*The treasure!*" cried the children, jumping out of their chairs.

"Nothing. Just like you, I was ready to quit. Imagine, a nice middle-aged woman digging up the garden in her nightgown. I tried to forget the whole thing, but it kept eating away at me. *Why* did someone put an X over that rosebush? Why did they hide the map behind the wallpaper? Suppose, I said, that where there used to be a rosebush someone had planted something else? I got out my determination and my shovel and I dug up the last two corners of the garden. There it was, three feet under a mess of phlox, a cigar box wrapped in foil and plastic. And inside that . . ."

"Jewels!" cried Annie Mae.

"Gold!" cried March.

"Dollar bills," said Aunt Emma. "Who's to say who buried them there? I would have given them to Old Snoot's family if he had any, which he didn't. It wasn't a huge fortune, but it's big enough to hire Miss Beefay's assistant, Miss Twinkle, to help with the pigs during the day. We'll just redouble our efforts. Unless you kids would rather pack it in?"

"Quit? Us?" said March.

"It'll mean working all day with the pigs as well as after supper. No more lounging at the lake," warned Aunt Emma.

"Who cares," said Josephine. "Are you sure that's how you want to spend your fortune?"

"Easy come, easy go," said Aunt Emma, and got to her feet. "As I see it, family honor is involved."

Bobo was picking up cups and smiling. "I hear someone got a raise at the Bunny Food Grocery Store," she said.

"What?" said Josephine.

"Never you mind," snapped Aunt Emma. "Let's go get to work." She gave Bobo a look over her shoulder. "Some folks have no romance in their souls."

Justice Prevails

The AGAC, LCCS, and BTWS were suspended for the rest of the summer. The children were so busy trying to teach the pigs to curtsy, and making the giant gum chain, they had time for little else. Such was the price of greatness. Occasionally, Uncle Bud would take them fishing and for a midnight dip, insisting that all work and no play was as bad as the other way around. If truth be told, the furious pace of rehearsals had become hard work, indeed.

Imogene still behaved proprietarily with her gum chain, and this caused arguments, but they were enjoyable, family-type squabbles.

"You are a poop," said Josephine.

"You are a double poop," said Imogene, and wondered what Edie Finkelstein would say if she ever called her a double poop. "Do you think you could visit me in New York this winter?"

"I will have to check my social calendar," said Josephine.

"Can't you fold more neatly?" complained Imogene.

"Why don't you fold and let me link for a change?" began Josephine. "You always get to link."

Nathan came in. "Aren't you ever going to come out and help rehearse the pigs? We still can't get them to bend on cue, and the contest is next week, you know."

"*All right!*" shouted both girls, and ran out to the barn.

When the day of the fair finally dawned, the pig act was still in an uncertain state. Sometimes the pigs curtsied and sometimes they didn't.

"I'm sorry," said Miss Beefay, who was going to the fair with the Reinsteins. "I did my best, and so did Miss Twinkle. I told you they were a bunch of dumb pigs."

"They're not dumb," said March. "And it's still a better act than last year's. If they do curtsy and don't just stand there," he added.

The children helped Uncle Bud load the pigs. Aunt Emma and Bobo were packing a picnic dinner. After a day at the fair, they were all going to have a picnic out in the cornfields as a goodbye party for Imogene. She was going home the next day.

The children decided they would all wear their sunglasses. Imogene was going to wear her scarf, too, but decided in the end not to upstage the Reinsteins. They hopped into the truck.

"Away we go!" called Aunt Emma gaily from her station wagon, and they were off.

The first thing the children did was help to get the pigs settled into their stalls. The pig talent contest wasn't until the afternoon, and they wanted the pigs to be calm and well rested for it. After that, the children would be free to explore the fair.

They left Bobo at the canning tent, where she was registering some strawberry preserves to be judged. They passed the handicrafts tent and then the oddity tent.

"What's that?" asked Imogene.

"Oh, you know," said Josephine. "People grow pumpkins that look like Richard Nixon, and stuff like that."

Beyond these tents loomed the Ferris wheel. The children hurried toward it.

They thought the wait for the pig talent contest would be agonizing, but with merry-go-rounds, the Ferris wheel, cotton candy, and candy apples, the time disappeared in a glorious whirl. Bud and Bobo had to remind them that they should be getting over to the stage.

They settled themselves into the middle row with Bud, Bobo, and Aunt Emma beside them. The Reinstein pigs were fourth on the program. The first act was supposed to be pigs jumping through a hoop. The pigs refused. One pig gnawed on the hoop. The audience roared. Next came a little girl who had dressed eight pigs as Snow White and the Seven Dwarfs. The audience applauded politely. The children agreed that this could hardly be called a display of talent. Next came a man with two pigs whom he claimed he had taught to laugh. He told the pigs jokes. The pigs oinked after the punch line. They also oinked during the punch line and throughout the joke. They were simply noisy pigs.

At last, March came out with their pigs. He had had the most luck getting the pigs to curtsy, so he had been elected to perform with the pigs onstage. He touched their backs, and one by one, glory be, if they didn't bend their legs, in a fit of sudden cooperation, and curtsy. The audience applauded madly. This was the best trick in years. The children glowed.

Josephine sighed in relief and checked the program to see when the Anderheimerhoopers would appear.

"Look," she whispered to the other children. "The Anderheimerhoopers aren't on the program. Aunt Emma, the Anderheimerhoopers haven't entered their pigs."

"I know," said Aunt Emma smugly. "Mrs. Anderheimerhooper found out from Dr. Cooper that the kids used her albino chipmunk to scare our pigs. It was bad enough losing her chipmunk, but when she found out that our corn had been damaged, she was so mad she pulled her kids' pigs from the contest. So, you see, there is justice in the universe, after all."

"But we're a cinch to win, then!" said Josephine. "Their pigs are the only real competition."

"Hush," a woman behind them said loudly. The next act was coming on.

"Ladies and gentlemen," said Mr. Ferguson, introducing his surprise last-minute entry. It was more than most people had ever heard him say. "I been training this pig nights as a little surprise for my wife. I named her Loulou in her honor. I trained Loulou to roll over. Roll over, Loulou." He tickled the pig. The pig just stood there. He tickled it again. The pig lay down. He tickled it once more. The pig wiggled a bit but refused to roll over. "Well, you'll have to take my word for it that she rolls over. I seen it a hundred times. This is one talented pig." And Mr. Ferguson took the pig offstage.

Applause was weak, except from the judge's booth, where someone was stamping her feet and shouting "Bravo!" Some of the audience left in disgust. It was pretty obvious who was going to win.

Sure enough, after the final entry, Loulou Ferguson got up on stage and announced that the winner was little Loulou Pig.

The Reinstein children hissed. Aunt Emma shushed them and pulled them out of the tent, while Bud and Bobo left to return the pigs to their stalls.

"But it's not *fair*," complained Josephine. "What happened to your justice in the universe?"

"Justice is a capricious lady," said Aunt Emma. "Look at it this way: that's one marriage saved and, well, there's always next year." But she bought them each a double-decker ice cream, because she didn't think it was fair, either.

"You mean there was no seedier side of life to begin with?" said Josephine, licking her cone. "Mr. Ferguson was sneaking out nights to train a pig because he wanted it to be a surprise for Loulou?"

"So it seems," said Aunt Emma. "How about another ride on the Ferris wheel?"

"Now we'll *never* be famous," said Josephine. "Things never work out the way you expect."

"Odd, isn't it?" said Aunt Emma. "We could go see if your ma won a ribbon for her preserves."

"*Odd!*" cried Imogene.

They stared at her.

"Odd!" she giggled gleefully.

"It's been too much for her," said Josephine in alarm. "Her little New York brains have given way."

"Odd. Odd. Odd," chortled Imogene. "What's odder than odd? What's a sure-fire oddity?"

"Oh, my," said Annie Mae, backing away.

"My gum chain!" she laughed. "*Our* gum chain. The oddity tent!"

"Lands' sake," said Aunt Emma.

"Can we enter it in time?" said Josephine, already running toward Aunt Emma's car, with the rest of them at her heels.

Aunt Emma made the dust fly down the road to the

farm. They threw the chain into the back seat and drove right up to the oddity tent, where people were still registering their oddities. Dr. Cooper was at the head of the line, registering something with Miss Hassenfeffer, who ran the oddity tent.

"Now isn't that something?" she said, examining his squash. "So big, and I do declare if it doesn't look just like our great and heroic President Lincoln."

Dr. Cooper beamed. It was clear he thought he had a good chance of winning. "It's something special, all right," he said.

"Of course, it's useful. You can cook it and eat it after the contest, can't you?" asked Miss Hassenfeffer.

"Oh, yes. Oh yes, I suppose you could," said Dr. Cooper.

"Hmmmm," said Miss Hassenfeffer. "Well, fill out this card and leave it on the table over there."

Next was a woman who had stuck old Christmas cards together into one lumpy, shellacked green-and-red mass. "How interesting!" said Miss Hassenfeffer with sincere admiration. "And so useless, too!"

"This," said the woman with dignity, "is a doorstop. Very useful. Very useful, indeed."

"Oh, dear," said Miss Hassenfeffer. "Nevertheless, it is a thing of beauty, my dear. Just fill out the card and leave it on the table over there."

Next came Miss Havary with her canary.

"Yes?" said Miss Hassenfeffer.

"I'd like to register my canary," said Miss Havary.

"This is the oddity tent, dear," said Miss Hassenfeffer.

"Yes, I know."

"Well, I don't see anything odd about your canary."

"He's an uncommonly fine one," argued Miss Havary.

"Yes, I'm sure he is, I'm sure he is, but he is not an uncommonly *odd* one," insisted Miss Hassenfeffer.

"You people are all the same," said Miss Havary, and stormed out.

Finally, there was only one man in front of them. "I've invented a plunger instrument," he said proudly.

"Not another one," groaned Miss Hassenfeffer.

"You can plunge and play 'She'll Be Comin' Round the Mountain,'" he explained.

"Well, that's practically useless, but not quite," said Miss Hassenfeffer cheerily. "Explain it in your own words on this card and leave it on the table over there."

Imogene felt her knees shake as their turn approached. They took the plastic off the gum chain.

"This," she announced in a husky voice, "is the world's largest gum chain."

"Magnificent," croaked Miss Hassenfeffer. You could see she was impressed. "What do you do with it?"

The children looked at each other blankly. "You just,

well, you just—" No one had ever asked Imogene this before. "You just *add* to it."

"And that's all?" asked Miss Hassenfeffer.

"Well, yes. It's an oddity, isn't it?" asked Josephine anxiously.

"Oh, undoubtedly that. Undoubtedly that," said Miss Hassenfeffer. "I was merely trying to determine whether it had some extraneous use."

"None," said March, who had never been smitten by gum-chain fever.

"I see," said Miss Hassenfeffer, pursing her lips thoughtfully. "Fill out this card and put it on the table over there."

Imogene felt discouraged. They filled out the card and walked out of the tent. "No one said you had to be able to *use* these things," she complained bitterly.

"Never mind," said Josephine. "Let's go get some cotton candy. They won't start judging for another half hour."

The children returned to the tent after a spin on the Ferris wheel. They dashed over to the gum chain and there, pinned to it, was a big blue ribbon.

"Congratulations, dearies, I was just filling in the winning certificates, suitable for framing. One for each of you, which is why it is taking me so long. We've never had so many names on a single entry before. I just knew it would win. It's so divinely useless." And she sighed

happily at the thought. "The local news wants to film a short segment. We were just going to try to find you and see if that would be agreeable."

The children beamed at her through their sunglasses. Whoever thought I would find fame and fortune in Iowa, Imogene thought. "Oh, quite agreeable," she answered for them.

After the newsmen were done with them, the Reinsteins went home to watch themselves on TV. It was wonderful. Imogene and Josephine each wondered if someone would have the good sense to discover them and make them stars. Then they went out to the picnic table in the cornfields and had supper. Afterwards, the children walked through the corn to find a place to set off fireworks.

"Next year we'll have two projects. Pigs and an oddity," said Josephine bossily. "Now, what's a good oddity?"

"How about the world's longest daisy chain?" asked Annie Mae.

"Too much like the gum chain," said Josephine.

"We could invent something," said March. "Like something that attracts worms so you don't have to dig them."

"Too useful," said Josephine. "Besides, digging worms is fun."

"Chocolate-covered dog biscuits," said Nathan.

"Shut up, Nathan," said everyone.

"We'll just have to think about it all winter," said Josephine. She turned to Imogene. "You'll have to think about it, too. You can write us your ideas and we will send you our gum wrappers."

Imogene was relieved. She had been worried that the Reinsteins would want to start their own gum chain. But no, clearly everyone knew that the gum chain belonged with Imogene whither she wandered, just as the agate collection belonged in Iowa, pigs on the farm, and the Statue of Liberty in New York. Then there was an explosion of light and color in the sky.

"You're going home tomorrow," said Josephine.

"I know," said Imogene.

Home

Goodbyes at airports are terrible things, so we will gloss right over the dreadful morning of the next day and not even hint at who might have cried or barked. Suffice it to say that Imogene got out at La Guardia Airport and was considerably cheered to see two beaming faces.

Life in New York began to take on a familiar getting-ready-for-school routine, with new clothes bought and notebooks and pencils looking raw and lovely in their unused state.

Edie Finkelstein returned from Camp Cherokee and she and Imogene met at Murdock's, their finances being at a low point.

"So they sent you back to camp," said Imogene, slurping her chocolate soda.

"Yes," said Edie. "I was a celebrity. The director wanted to ignore the whole incident, but my cabin held Edie Finkelstein Night. I told the whole story by flashlight."

"My gum chain is famous in Iowa," said Imogene.

"Yeah, I know. I got your letter," said Edie.

"Speaking of letters," said Imogene. She pulled out her first letter from her cousins and read it as they sipped. "They say hi to you. And, oh no, the Anderheimer-hoopers claim they are entering something in the oddity contest next year."

"I'm glad your gum chain won," said Edie.

"You're a true friend," said Imogene. "Look, they all signed it."

Edie looked puzzled. "What's that?" she said, pointing to the bottom of the page. Among the signatures there was a paw print.

"Nathan!" Imogene giggled. "Wait a sec, there's a P.S. on the back of the page." She read it and jumped up. "Come on," she said, grabbing Edie by the elbow.

"Where are we going?" asked Edie.

"Downtown," said Imogene, pulling Edie out the door. "There's a statue we have to see."